KILLER CRESCENT

REBELS AND PSYCHOS BOOK ONE

LEIGH KELSEY

Rebels and Psychos is RH, which means Rebel doesn't have to choose between her many lovers. This series contains mature scenes intended for adult readers.

This book was written, produced, and edited in the UK where some spelling, grammar and word usage will vary from US English.

Copyright © Leigh Kelsey 2021

All rights reserved. No part of this publication may be reproduced or transmitted in any form or by any means, electronic or mechanical, without the prior written permission of the author

This is a work of fiction. Names, characters, places and incidents either are products of the author's imagination or are used fictitiously. Any resemblance to actual events or locales or persons, living or dead, is entirely coincidental.

The right of Leigh Kelsey to be identified as author of this work has been asserted by her in accordance with the Copyright, Designs and Patents Act 1988

www.leighkelsey.co.uk

Want an email when new books release - and four freebies?
Join here by clicking here

Or chat with me in my Facebook group: Leigh Kelsey's Paranormal Den

Cover by Everly Yours Cover Designs

Created with Vellum

BLURB

If a secret wolf society thinks they can take me down, they've got another thing coming. There's a reason they call me Graves.

It's not my fault I'm a psychopath. What else would happen to someone who witnessed her sister's murder? Without magic in my arsenal like the rest of my family, I have to rely on other methods: sharp knives, stealth, and killer instincts. And hey, killing pays the bills.

I've been a magical dud all my life, the black sheep of the Falcon witch line, but my family are liars. When I'm stalking my next victim under the blood moon, I sprout fur, sharp teeth, and a fuzzy tail.

It turns out I'm a dual-blood, both a witch and a wolf, and now I'm on the radar of the Crescent Club, one of three ancient societies of witches, wolves, and vampires. I'm given two options: move into Blake Hall, a dark gothic mansion in the middle of nowhere, or get my power stripped.

Luckily, I have five dangerous psycho mates on my side: dominant alpha Dean, insane vampire Slasher, sweet bookish Brannigan, my silent shadow Hugh, and cruel Edison who rejects me but can't deny our chemistry.

Killer Crescent is a paranormal romance with psycho men, a badass FMC, twisted romance, and lots and lots of bloodlust. Secret societies, killer wolves, dangerous vamps, and cunning witches lurk in these pages, but all of them will meet the sharp end of Rebel Falcon's knife. This book is medium burn, with moderate heat, and multiple love interests.

NOTE

Both the heroine and the love interests of this series are complete psychos. They love murdering and violence and stuff that'll make your stomach curdle. Proceed with caution.

These psychos also love their sex rough and hot, but don't try any of this at home unless you know how to do it in a safe, consensual manner. And ALWAYS do your research first (something as basic as hair pulling could slip a disc in your partner's spine.)

This book also contains mentions of abuse and assault that could trigger some readers.

If you're good with blood, gore, and dirty steam, read on!

NOTE, PART 2

You're gonna want to read the footnotes.

1

"Here Dicky, Dicky, Dicky," I murmured, crouching in the long grass as I waited for my target's jogging steps to reach the dark corner of forest where I planned to ambush him.

Dicky Lawson was about as big a douche as his name suggested. A high powered lawyer and a cocky piece of shit, he'd pissed off a list of people at least a mile long. Lucky me, one of them had paid me to make him disappear. Or as I liked to call it, make him go *night night*. Obviously I took my job *very* seriously.

"Ah, there you are," I whispered, grinning as Dicky jogged into view, his long legs eating up the dirt path and a strip of sweat bisecting his blue T-shirt, just visible in the dimming light. He wasn't one of those joggers who blasted music in their ears; he liked to hear the *nature* around him, to soak up the full benefit of the *experience*. I knew because he'd posted those exact words on his Facebook profile a few days ago. And people said *I* was a psychopath; weirdos who exercised for fun were the real psychos. You never knew what they were going to do next. Bench press a bus for shits and giggles? It could happen.

Watching Dicky cross the dark clearing, I wiped a finger clean on my clothes—all black because it hid the bloodstains; my entire murder wardrobe was made up of jet, onyx, ink, and sable—and shoved said finger in my eye, giving it a good poke before I moved onto the next one until tears streamed down my cheeks. I'm sure there were easier and better ways to achieve the same result, but this worked.

Patting my hoodie to be sure check my knives were there —all present and accounted for—I let out a loud sobbing sniffle and cried out, "Pooky? Pooky, where are you?"

In a frantic rush, I jumped out from behind the tree, swinging my gaze across the clearing, and 'spotting' Dicky. "Oh, please tell me you've seen a dog around here," I begged, twigs and bracken crunching under my heavy boots as I ran up to him, and sobbed extra loudly as I clutched his biceps. They were annoyingly well defined biceps for a dickhead lawyer and a night jogger. Shame he wasn't my type; too full of himself, too slimy. "He's about this high, and white with shaggy fur. Oh, I don't know what I'll do if he's gotten lost. Or—" I produced a shattered sob, and a damn good one if I said so myself. "Or if he's gotten onto the road and a car—"

"I'm sure he's around here somewhere," Dicky assured me, but with his chest puffed up and a gleam in his eye I didn't quite like. Like he'd help find the dog so he could brag about it and feel good about himself, not because a helpless little dog might get knocked down. The *monster*. I was glad I was about to kill him.

"You th-think?" I gasped, blinking more tears down my face. Fuck, my eyes were stinging, but the bloodshot look probably added a touch of authenticity to the role.

"I'll help you look for him," Dicky offered, still puffed up with purpose and righteousness as he stepped closer, probably about to offer some halfhearted reassurance until he walked into my knife. Whoops.

"What—" he gasped, but I whipped my blade up and sliced through his throat before he could utter anything else. It was a tidy, quiet job. One of my best, actually, but my favourites were the chaotic, bloody ones.

"Sorry, Dicky," I said with a laugh at his stunned stare as his body crashed to the leaf-strewn ground at my feet. "But you really shouldn't have represented that murderer. The girl's family is *not* pleased with you."

I knelt and wiped my knife on his sweaty top, scanning the clearing to make sure we were alone. I'd just break down into traumatised sobs and say I'd found him like this anyway; it had worked before. Why would a twenty-year-old, pink-haired girl with a heart-shaped face and big, blue doe eyes *possibly* kill someone? *Obviously*, I was an innocent bystander.

I rolled my eyes, a scoff in my throat. Although ... people's assumptions had gotten me away from the scene safely more than a handful of times, so I was happy for people to think I was a sweet, innocent little girl.

After all, I *was* a sweet, innocent little girl. When I wasn't murdering people to pay the bills, anyway.

"Don't worry," I told Dicky, reaching into my pocket to pull out a lightweight sheet of silk that had cost me a bloody fortune, spreading it out over his body. And voila! Body magically disappeared. Well, not really, it was just hidden under the camouflage silk, but now passersby wouldn't start screaming about a little bit of blood and a dead body. People could be so dramatic sometimes. "I already took out your buddy, so you and the murderer can hang out in hell together. Or wherever else you end up," I added. I'd mused about it often, where people went when they died. It was a recurring thought given my line of work, but I'd never find out the answer. Not until I died anyway, and I'd yet to meet anyone crazy enough to try and kill me.

Everyone knew you didn't fuck with Rebel Falcon AKA Graves. Well, everyone but the witch community, and especially my family—the Falcon witch line—but they were all assholes anyway. *Where's your magic, Rebel? Cast a spell, Rebel. You're such a failure, Rebel.* Blah. I'd got the final word though, and my dear cousin Antonella had left the pretty bloodstain in the hallway to prove it. Or at least I thought she had; those bastards could have gotten it magically removed, but I hoped they still remembered the vital lesson: don't piss me off, or I get stabby.

The sun had dropped by the time I got Dicky rolled up in the silk and made sure no one was watching as I hauled him by his feet into the trees, swearing up a storm at his weight. I trained whenever I could, making my body strong, my reflexes deadly fast, but dragging a two hundred pound man was difficult for any woman. Even Wonder Woman would struggle to dispose of a body.

"There," I panted, rolling him under a bush and giving him a kick for good measure. Sweat rolled off my forehead, and my shirt was stuck to me, but I was almost done and ready to go home, sink into an extra-bubbly bath, and drink champagne from the bottle. I might have lived in a modest one-bedroom flat in Birmingham, but I had expensive tastes in booze, and my little killing hobby—well, my very serious murder career—could pay for a few luxuries a week. Anything too crazy, and I'd have nothing left for rent. Killing people was not as lucrative a job as people believed; there just weren't enough people around to kill. Criminals tended to take out their own enemies, which was just rude—some people were out here trying to earn a living.

"This is your fault, Dicky," I muttered, kicking his legs again even though he was stone cold dead and had done nothing to me personally.

I always got antsy around the full moon, and I could see it rising now, tainted strangely pink, like the moon had got her hands bloody killing someone, too. It was a witchy time of the month, when all the magical bastards gathered and cast spells for good health and prosperity and everything else that made me gag. Everything else I'd been excluded from for as long as I could remember. I was a dud, a failure of the powerful Falcon line, and they hadn't let me forget it for a damn minute.

But who needed magic when you had sharp, pointy objects?

"Right, Dicky?"

I glared down at the camouflaged lump. "Well, that's just rude, there's no need to ignore me."

Yes, I was talking to a corpse. I never said I was sane.

Pinkish light bathed the ground as I gathered my bag from where I'd stashed it and changed into non-bloody clothes—also a lovely shade of ebony—before I pulled back the silk sheet to take some pretty incriminating photos. Thank fuck I wasn't hooked up to the cloud.

Dicky's grey face and the bloody gash in his throat winged its way through the airwaves to my client, with the message: *Dead as a doornail. You're very welcome, good sir, no need to thank me, just wire the rest of the £20,000 into my bank.*

I got back one word, which was a bit stand-offish, but that was clients for you. They couldn't muster a single manner, let alone mann*ers*. The text just read, *Done*.

A quick check of my bank had a grin splitting my face.

"I'm eating well tonight, Dicky. Chinese *and* Indian. Ooh, maybe pizza too." A groan rattled my throat to match my rumbling stomach. "Garlic bread, with cheese and herbs. Fresh doughnuts. Oh! I want a whole box of Chupa Chups lollies. In cola flavour."

Dicky didn't reply, but I'd honestly have been worried if he had. So far that hadn't happened to any of my corpses, but with magic in the world, you never knew. Luckily, I kept a taser in my pack just for zombies. And for targets who got touchy feely; those got tasered in the dick. Or the tit; turns out I was alluring to all genders.[1]

I logged out of my bank and hit my number one speed-dial, winding a strand of bubblegum hair around my finger. "Hiii, Julius."

"Oh, no, not you," he groaned, seconds away from putting down the phone.

"I have a present for you," I cut in before he could end the call. "It's worth five grand for you."

"I hate you," Julius grumbled, dour as always. "Give me the address."

I grinned, and told him where to find dear old Dicky, bouncing on my toes with excitement. I'd found Julius by accident when he was apprenticing to one of my first, waayyyy more expensive cleaners, and we'd started a heart-warming friendship of me nagging him to strike out on his own and him giving me the same level of glare as a cat being woken from a two-hour nap. Now, he got a much bigger cut, and I got bodies disposed of cheaper. Win-win. Plus, Julius had a sweet tooth, unlike his previous employer. I just didn't trust people who hated cookies. It was unnatural. Like jogging for fun.

"You're my favourite," I told Julius, and put the phone down before his groan could finish. "Right, then. Time to go home." I grinned; I could already taste the prawn balls and doughnuts.[2]

I reached my arms up, stretching out the kinks from dragging Dicky, and bent to retrieve my expensive silk sheet when pain lanced through my middle, stopping me. The vicious pang sent me crashing to my knees in the undergrowth, a gasp tearing up my throat. "What ... the fuck?"

It felt like lightning had struck, like a hot poker had been shoved through my back, but I collapsed onto my side and reached back ... and found nothing. No wound, no sword, not even a measly little kitchen knife. "Kittens," I swore. I didn't believe in god, but I did believe in kittens, and right now having a little furry face pressed to mine would make me feel a whole lot better about the pain shifting through my insides.

A bone broke in my leg, and I screamed, loud enough for birds to take flight from the trees above. Loud enough to draw attention to myself. Thank fuck Dicky was still concealed, or we'd have had a much bigger problem. At least I couldn't be arrested for my bones snapping in two, which they continued to do, sending cracks of agony up through my legs, and then down my arms. Limp and useless, I fell forward so fast that dirt coated my tongue. "Ugh." I spat it out, but there was no removing the gross taste on my tongue, and I swore my sense of taste doubled, and then tripled, just to piss me off. I gagged, my stomach twisted up on itself, and screamed through clenched teeth as my spine realigned—

"Oh, no," I rasped, as I got a sneaking suspicion of what was happening. But it made no damn sense. I was from a witch line, not a furry, snarly beast line. "Please—" I panted, as the plates in my spine shifted. "Let me—be a—kitten—shifter."

But there was no such thing. There were only witches, vampires, and wolves. And the chances of me being a secret vamp just discovering her bat form were... Yeah, pathetically slim.

The pain erupted like a fire doused in petrol, and my back arched, my body twisted as I panted and screamed. No one had come to investigate the screaming—that was either good or bad. But Julius would be turning up soon, and I had no idea how to explain this. How a dud of a witch was suddenly *shifting*.

Deep bronze magic flashed in the corner of my vision, and the pain washed away, replaced by a sensitivity that was almost as bad. Too many sounds competed for my attention, condensing into a droning buzz that gave me an instant headache, and the smells of dirt and trees and Dicky's blood shoved up my nose until I gagged. And that was *before* I tried to shove up to my feet, and claws gouged the dirt under me, the earth rubbing against the pads of *paws*.

They weren't cute, ickle kitten paws, either—I knew without hunting down a reflection that I was a wolf, my legs too long to be a kitty, and my fur the deep greyish black of the Silver Sable wolf line. The wolf line my mum must have had a dalliance with in her youth. Oh, she was in *so* much trouble. Not that she'd have to deal with the family finding out; she was long gone, killed by a spell gone wrong when I was two. But I knew our family would strike her from the family tree in a petty rage. Witches were stupid that way.

They were so focussed on keeping the lines pure, on maintaining the strength and power of our magic, they didn't see they were becoming scarily like Death Eaters. *Some* lines were progressive and liberal. The Falcon line was not.

And I was the illegitimate love-child of a witch and a wolf.

Perfect.

Good thing I never saw those fuckers anymore, and I had my own content, murdery life. But that life was quickly becoming a sack of shit; now that I was stuck with a wolf form, I'd have no choice but to deal with this shifting agony once a month. This was *not* how I wanted to spend my Saturday night.

Although ... a wicked thought occurred to me.

There was a rival assassin who'd always irritated me to no end. As a wolf, I could piss on all his clothes. People tended to get judgy when you did that in human form. *Why are you taking your clothes off, Rebel? Why are you squatting over those expensive shirts, Rebel? Why are you giving me a death stare why you vengefully pee, Rebel?*

People were so annoying with their societal rules. In *my* society, anyone could take revenge in any way they deemed, even if that involved a teensy splash of urine. And a wolf form. Fuck, I had a *wolf form* now, and I had no idea what to do until the moon set and the sun rose.

Did moons even set? I had no idea. I was a failure of a witch and an epic badass of a hitlady—I didn't know moon phases and what parts of the forest to avoid and which wolves not to pick fights with. Kittens, I didn't even know which wolves were the *alphas*. Knowing my luck, I'd piss off the biggest, baddest alpha. But then I could just stab him when I was back in human form. That thought cheered me up; I did like to get stabby and all creative with bloody patterns. I'd once carved Twilight Sparkle into some gross dude's back. She was the prettiest, bloodiest, goriest *My Little Pony* I'd ever seen.

Focus, Rebel! I was adjusting to the thick haze of scents

and the noisy clamour, able to pick out individual sounds and isolate scents. And now I wasn't completely overwhelmed, I needed to get out of here before Julius turned up. I liked the guy well enough, but I didn't want him knowing a secret about me. And this seemed like the sort of thing I should keep secret. Dual-bloods weren't a thing around here. Maybe in the super liberal covens and packs down in London, but chances were I'd get chased out of Birmingham with torches and pitchforks. Witches were fucking crazy.

Must be where I got it from.

Padding tentatively across the ground, and marvelling at how sensitive my paws were, how the wind ruffling through my fur felt as amazing as having my hair stroked, I approached dead Dicky and snapped around with my new, unwieldy jaws until teeth closed around soft silk.

I reeeeally hoped no one caught me now, because having to explain why a wolf was carrying around a sheet was not going to be easy. Unless they thought they'd misseen and were going crazy. It happened to the best of us. Craziness, that is. My own mind broke five years ago while I hid under my sister's bed as her boyfriend burst into the room in a rage. But I didn't like to think about that day, about her soft pleas and his deep growls and the blood afterward…

Sometimes I thought that was where my obsession with the red, gushy stuff had started. But I'd always enjoyed breaking my cousins' noses and watching the crimson flow, so maybe I'd always been a little fucked up. It was fun breaking people's noses; you should try it.

My ears twitched at footsteps a few paths away, and I rolled my enchanted cloth into as small a bundle as I could manage with paws and jaws—hey, that rhymed; I should start a band called that!—and snapped it up in my teeth, trotting away.

Well, I'd *planned* to trot away, all elegance and powerful muscle. But I *might* have swerved and stumbled across a few roots, and *maybe* walked snout-first into a tree before I found a hiding place behind a thick bush—*don't snort at thick bush, don't snort at thick bush*—and watched Julius stomp his way into the clearing. He sighed huffily at the sight of Dicky but snapped on a pair of gloves anyway.

Leaving him to his job, I carefully picked up my legs and tiptoed away. Tip-pawed away? The air smelled amazing away from Dicky's copper and rot scent, and I gulped it down, tasting oak trees and rich earth and ... was that a squirrel?

I groaned, and the sound emerged as a low, rumbling growl. My mouth filled with saliva. *Don't chase the squirrel, Rebel,* I warned myself. But I was too wolfy to ignore that enticing scent, and I took off at a sprint, wind whistling past my black and silver fur as I finally got the hang of these loping legs and strange paws. My wolf form was fucking awesome, and I let out an overjoyed yip. Shame I couldn't film myself; this would make an epic TikTok. One minute, cute, innocent pink-haired girl, the next—BAM!—super vicious killer. Well, I was a super vicious killer no matter what, but they didn't need to know that. Shifting could be my party trick. My once a month, fun as fuck party trick. If it wouldn't get me kicked, punched, and screamed at, I'd make a game of shifting in front of unsuspecting humans just to see the looks on their dumbstruck faces.

Wait, no, back to the squirrel. Mmm, smelled tasty.

I ran head-first at the tree the squirrel scarpered up, the delectable fucker disappearing into a nook in the trunk and poking out its little face to give me a look that quite clearly said, *ha-ha, can't catch me now, big scary wolfie.*

Next time, Bitesize, I promised, but all that came out was a low snarl.

I whipped my head around as I caught another scent. Bigger, but still fucking delicious. I gave the squirrel a toothy grin and raced off—and skidded to a halt, and forced myself to turn back. I picked up my forgotten silk sheet, and raced back toward that enticing scent.

I slowed to a prowl a few paces away, the thrill of the hunt singing through my blood as I peered through a bush into someone's back garden and—

No, I hissed at my wolf. I mentally rolled up a newspaper and bopped her on the nose. *No hunting, bad wolfie.*

The mouth-watering scent was a beautiful grey *cat*, and no way in heaven, hell, or earth was I hunting a kitty. So I tucked my tail between my legs and skulked back into the forest. There was plenty of time to go squirrel hunting before the sun came up. If I was lucky, Julius would have cleared all signs of my murder antics by then, and I'd be able to go home to the nice chunk of money sat in my bank account.

Unless a human saw me and phoned the police—or the RSPCA.

Then I'd be shoved into the back of a van and shipped off to fuck knows where. Imagining the looks on their faces when they opened the van doors to find a naked, human woman was almost worth getting caught.

But no way in hell would I survive *that* questioning. And I'd definitely be on the witches' radar then. There'd be no keeping the Falcon line away from me. And life as I knew it would all go to shit.

Better not get caught, then.

The wind ruffled through my fur as I stalked back through the forest, letting the sounds and smells wash over me, and taking it all in. This was my life now. I snorted through my nose at the absurdity of it. If I'd been in human form I'd have been singing *yo-ho, yo-ho, it's a werewolf's life for me.*

But as I passed through a clearing and the pink light of the blood moon fell on my fur again, I could have sworn magic rushed up through me. *Witch* power.

Not good.

Not good at all.

2

I'd been home just long enough to take a scalding shower and gorge on a box of doughnuts slathered in chocolate and unicorn sprinkles[1] when a heavy knock interrupted my peace.

I brought the last doughnut with me, cradled to my chest, as I wrenched the door to my flat open and glared at the bastard who'd dared to disturb me. "You better have a *damn* good reason for knocking, buddy, or I'll fuck you up so hard even your ass will be crying."

The forty-something guy standing on my flat's doorstep stared at me with narrowed eyes. "What?"

"I don't know," I huffed, nibbling on the doughnut. "I barely slept last night okay, give me a break." Try not sleeping *at all* because I was too busy being a wolf, but this guy didn't need to know that.

Make that this suuuper hot, mouth-watering silver fox. Holy *fuck*, what had I done to deserve this sexy specimen at my front door? I let my eyes pour over him, from the silver hair falling around his rugged face in debonair strands, to his stubbled, square jaw, to his broad shoulders and tight fitting tweed suit. I tried not to linger *too* long on the cupid's bow of his seriously-begging-me-to-kiss-them lips.

"Helloooo, daddy," I purred, leaning against the doorframe and batting my eyelashes at him. "What brings you to my door? Need a cup of sugar? Want a tumble in the sheets? The answer's yes to either, just so you know."

"I'm from Blake Hall," he replied, all stern and serious, like I ought to know what that was. He looked all sexy bristling and angry, his whiskey-brown eyes hard with a warning I gleefully ignored. "The correctional home for wayward and criminal supernaturals," he went on, his jacket straining as he crossed his strong arms over his chest.

I gave him a wide-eyed stare. *Criminal? Who, me? Not me, sir.*

"Oh, no," I breathed. "Has someone escaped? Is that why you're here—to ask me if I've seen them in the area?" I batted my lashes, giving him a sultry smile. "I haven't seen anyone, sir, but I promise I'd tell you if I had. I'm a good girl, see."

His mouth thinned, and he shoved past me, rudely stalking into my living room with heavy footsteps.

"Hey!" I complained as he walked across my pretty mermaid-scale rug without taking his shoes off. He had the nerve to sink onto my couch, manspreading and looking annoyingly at home there. Huffing, I took mental inventory of the weapons I had stashed in the room, and lost count when I hit twenty-three. More than enough.

"Sit down," he growled, and the sound was so powerful —so *alpha*—that the new wolfie part of me sat up and took notice. The human part of me bristled, already planning his murder. Except for my pussy. She had other plans, and explained them to me with very insistent throbs. It was a good plan. I was listening.

"This is my house," I argued, planting my hands on my hips and staying by the door. "You don't get to order me around, no matter how fancy *your* house is."

His stare flattened with exasperation. I wanted to push him, to see what happened when he broke. But something told me that would take a long, lonnnnng time to happen, and I didn't have the patience for it. Today. Maybe if he came back tomorrow when I'd had a full night's sleep, I might feel differently.

I didn't like the tiny smile at the edge of his mouth, or the way he stretched his legs out on my rug, confident and assured.

"Are you aware the supernatural community has a coven of seers on hand to alert them whenever someone develops new magic?"

F. U. C. Double K.

"What do you want?" I demanded, cutting through the small talk as I slammed the door shut. I didn't want my very human neighbours witnessing this.

I wrapped my arms around my middle to disguise palming the tiny throwing knife from my leggings waistband. He was so unbelievably hot, but I'd still put a knife through his heart if he tried to hurt me.

That damned smirk kicked up higher on his stubbled face, and my clit throbbed. *Not the fucking time*, I hissed at my dripping pussy. He was probably here to kill me, or arrest me, and I was *not* getting turned on by his threatening aura.

Except, I so *was* getting turned on by his threatening aura.

I probably needed counselling for that.

"*I* don't want anything, Miss Falcon," he replied, smugly

calm. That term fit him well—smugly calm. The smugly calm bastard.

"Son of a bitch," I hissed at his reply. He knew my name —and my witch line. I was so screwed, and not in the way my pulsing clit wanted.

"But the seers foresaw that your magic is volatile," he added, watching me like a hawk. Or a predatory wolf.

"I don't even *have* magic," I grumbled, stalking over to the couch to sit too damned close to him. Hoooly fuck, he smelled good, like woodsy herbs and spice. Was that peppercorn? I resisted the urge to lean in and lick him, just to be sure. "Ask anyone," I went on, tightening my hold on my little knife. "Everyone knows I'm a dud."

His smirk deepened, and I swayed towards him as he faced me full-on. Damn, his aura, his bearing, his scent ... everything pulled me towards him. I wanted to climb onto his lap and ride him like a rodeo, and my muscles ached with the force of holding back. "You *were* a dud, but you must have taken a stroll in the moonlight last night." The smirk became a knowing grin. "And your wolf form unlocked your hidden witch powers."

My mouth fell open, and I forgot to be glarey. "So *that's* what happened."

His smug grin appeared here to stay. I wanted to kiss it off his face just because that cockiness was too damn tempting, but ... that might have been defeating the object. "It is. And it leaves us with a problem. Your magic is volatile, and you have no idea how to control it *or* your wolf form. Wolf aggression could turn a sweet girl into a ruthless killer."

I giggle-snorted.

Sweet girl? Aw, he was being *nice* to me.

"I'm serious," he growled, full of dominance and alphaness. I shuddered, tingly and hot all over, and shuffled an inch closer without fully meaning to. "You're dangerous now."

"I was dangerous before," I said with a laugh, and booped him on the nose.

His expression went dark with warning, all deliciously violent. Fuck, I'd love to fight with him. The two of us rolling on the floor, hot and sweaty, flashing knives and sharp canine teeth...

"Miss Falcon," Mr Hot and Threatening growled, and I blinked my fantasies free.

"Hmm? Sorry, were you saying something? I was having a *very* good daydream. Would you like to know what was happening in it?" I gave him a winning smile.

"No," he replied flatly, his low voice sending shivers down my spine. "Pay attention; this is important."

I sat cross-legged and straight-backed on the sofa, twisting to face him with what I hoped was an attentive expression. I might have thrust my chest out a tad. Sue me. "Attention paid," I promised. "Go ahead, Sexy Sir."

I could see his irritation mounting, but he reined it in. That was no fun. "You've been put on a watch list of dangerous supernaturals, which gives you two choices. You can come back to Blake Hall with me, where we can monitor your power—and your shifts—and help you master both."

"You can master anything you want," I purred—and then blinked at the way his eyes darkened to full black. "Ah. I said that out loud, didn't I?"

"Yes," he growled, leaning towards me as if he couldn't help himself, either.

"What's my other choice?" I asked. "You said I had two."

"You'll be forced to register, and your magic will be stripped."

"Yeah, no thank you," I replied instantly. I might not have known this magic existed, or have particularly wanted it, but it was mine. I wasn't giving it up. Plus, the idea of becoming a badass witch and turning up at a Falcon family dinner, blasting the whole thing to pieces with my immense power ... that sounded like fun. Like justice and revenge and all the other things I loved.

"Good." He nodded, standing in a controlled rush. Damn, the way he moved ... I knew he'd be amazing in bed. "Pack your things, we'll leave in ten minutes."

Laughter rushed up my throat and burst out in a bright sparkle of sound. "Sorry to hurt your feelings, but I'm not moving in with you."

"You come, or you get stripped," he replied, arms crossed over his chest. His poor tweed jacket strained at the seams.

"If you want me to come..." I gave him a suggestive smile, getting slowly to my feet and prowling closer. "I'm not going to argue. But I'm not moving into your fancy-ass hall."

"Then you lose your magic." He shrugged, as if he couldn't care less.

I scowled. Of course there was option C—kill him. It was a shame he had to die, but needs must. I tensed my muscles to end him—

But no matter how I held the knife in my hand, I couldn't bring my arm to swing it, couldn't plunge the blade into his throat. I couldn't even *try* to hurt him, and I glared at my hand as if it had betrayed me. Because it fucking had!

"What have you done to me?" I growled at the sexy bastard, throwing aside my tiny knife so hard it embedded in the wall. I stalked back to the couch, digging under the cushions until I found a blowpipe. Knives were my preferred weapons, but I was a tad annoyed with my steel right now. Yet when I set the pipe to my mouth, I couldn't find the air to fill it, couldn't get my lips to purse.

Hot and Threatening started chuckling, a low, sexy sound that sent heat throughout my body, building into a throaty laugh that filled my quiet front room.

"*What?*" I demanded, throwing the pipe aside too. Useless thing.

"Are you trying to kill me?" he asked, still laughing. His brown eyes sparkled, his posture easing.

"Yes!" I snarled. "Why won't you die already?"

He moved suddenly and without warning, and I didn't move fast enough to escape him. A hot, broad hand closed around my throat, and the groan that rattled my throat was pure sex and wanton need.

Whoops. I definitely needed counselling.

"Because, Miss Falcon," he said with great relish, "you cannot kill your mate."

3

Mr Hot and Threatening dipped his face closer, sharp teeth scraping my ear and sending a cool rush of tingles down my spine.

"Wait—" I said breathlessly. "Mate? What?"

His laugh shuddered all the way through my body until I was uncomfortably hot, my nipples hard enough to cut glass. "You're drawn to me. You find me irresistible. You want me to take you against the wall so hard you forget your own name."

Well. Now that he mentioned it...

"Because you're my mate," he went on, sounding smug. "And your instincts are running wild."

I shoved him back, scowling at the strength I felt beneath his jacket, his chest made of solid muscle. Muscle I wanted to lick every inch of—

Dammit. Get it together, Rebel, he's trying to trick you into going home with him—and not for a fun roll in the sheets. For a ... what? Dangerous magic training program? It sounded like probation, and I'd done that once already, had no interest in doing it again.

"Hang on," I said, my lips pulling up in a smirk as something occurred to me. "Mate bonds are a two way street, which means *you*, Sexy Sir, are as drawn to *me*. You're the one who wants to fuck me against the wall; admit it."

I set my hands on my hips and gave him a sassy look, watching his eyes darken to deep brown, veined with black. Ooh, did mine look like that when I got horny? I wanted to run for the mirror, but this was too alluring to walk away from. I kinda wanted to see if he *would* throw me up against the wall and have his way with me.

"You can't admit it," I taunted, grinning. "But you know I'm right. The big bad alpha is desperate for the cute, ickle wolfie." Even witches and vampires had mate bonds, but wolf ones were especially powerful.

He raised a thick eyebrow. "You call yourself cute?"

"Yeah," I replied, like he was stupid. "If I don't, who will? Other people?" I made a gagging sound. "I hate other people. Unless they're hot. Or delivering pizza and doughnuts."

Exasperation crept across his face, and he took a step back. "Pack your bags. Unless you want your magic stripped —and your ability to shift along with it—you're coming back to Blake Hall with me."

I closed the distance and draped myself across his strong, powerful body, batting my lashes up at him. "You should know I only sleep on the right side of the bed, I don't do mornings, and I like *long, hot* ... showers."

I cursed as his hand closed around my throat again, and I swore the tips of his fingers were edged with sharp claws. Fuuuuck, he must have been powerful to partially shift the day after the moon. I swooned.

"You'll have your own room. Far away from mine."

"Aww, that's not nice. I'm your mate, remember."

"I'm trying to forget," he deadpanned, but he was such a lying liar because his hand flexed on my throat, and his eyes were still threaded with darkness.

"But imagine all the fun we could have if we shared a room," I purred, testing his hold on my neck by darting forward to drag my tongue up the column of his throat, an *mmm* in the back of my throat at his taste. I didn't actually want to share a room with him—no, it'd be impossible to hide my day job from him if he had eyes on me all the time —but I reeeeally wanted his cock. Maybe because he was my mate and affecting me with all this mate bond magic, or maybe because he was older and growly and everything about him screamed *dominant*.

"Miss Falcon," he warned, wrenching me away from his chest. "This is ridiculous."

"You taste amazing," I said, licking my lips just to see his reaction.

His hand left my throat, and I pouted, sticking out my bottom lip—but his fingers twisted in my hair and dragged me close enough to see the threat and warning in his eyes. It sent shivers of pleasure up and down my body, and I took advantage of our renewed closeness to rub up against him like an amorous cat. Well, wolf.

"If you won't pack, I'll do it for you," he said, all low and rumbly.

"Nope, stay right here." I rolled my hips against his, my pussy dragging across the hard length of his erection through his trousers.

"Fuck," he rasped, tightening his grip on my hair. "Could you behave for one fucking second, Rebel?"

"I doubt it," I replied, grabbing handfuls of his ass so I could fit closer to his cock.

"Do you *want* to be stripped of your power?" he growled,

ducking his face to scrape sharp canines against my throat. My whole body went hot and cold at once, shivers rushing through me and my pussy throbbing an insistent plea.

"Stripped of my clothes? Yes. Stripped of my power? No. I'll kill anyone who even tries to take it from me," I promised, cold hard murder in my eyes.

Hot and Threatening drew back, seeing the seriousness in my gaze, the razor sharp madness right behind it. Interest sharpened his whiskey eyes. "Have you ever killed someone before? It's not as easy as you might think, Miss Falcon."

I snorted. I couldn't help it. "You know my name, but you haven't looked into my record?" I tutted. "That's not very thorough of you, Sexy Sir."

"Garrick," he corrected. "My name's Dean Garrick."

"Dean," I repeated, drawing it out on my tongue. It suited him, and I liked it.

"Garrick," he corrected, disapproval flattening his mouth and drawing my gaze to that tempting cupid's bow. "What do you mean, your record?"

I snorted again. "Idiot alpha. You're too reliant on seers; you should have checked my paperwork, too. Don't worry, Dean." I patted his stubbled cheek. "You can't be super hot *and* amazingly clever. Unless you're me." I winked, and shivered with pleasure at the low growl in his throat.

"So you have killed someone," he surmised. "And were stupid enough to get caught. So *not* amazingly clever after all."

I definitely shouldn't have gotten even more turned on at the taunt in his voice. I shrugged, a feline movement. "Maybe I just got caught that once. Maybe there have been lots and lots of times I haven't gotten caught." I ducked in to scrape my teeth across his jaw. "Or maybe I'm just lying to get a reaction out of you."

Dean made a throaty sound, pushing me away—and letting go, to my displeasure. "Stay here, get stripped of your power—it makes no odds to me."

"You're not even a teensy bit worried about me, as your mate?"

"No," he replied without blinking.

I crossed my arms over my chest as he straightened his tweed jacket where I'd pawed at it, and strolled past me towards the door. My mouth fell open in outrage. He was leaving? After all that sexual tension? *Without* the promised wall fucking? Well, that was rude.

And there was the minor complication that if I let him walk out, some bastards would hunt me down to strip my witch magic. *And* my shifting powers. I'd kill them all, obviously, but it would get boring pretty fast. I'd have to stay hidden, change my appearance to stay off their radar ... and honestly that sounded so dull and exhausting.

"Fine!" I sighed as Dean opened the door, choosing to ignore the victorious smirk he threw over his shoulder. "What kind of wardrobe are we talking? Spring? Summer? Should I bring my bikini, or is there no pool at this fancy-ass hall?"

Dean's brows drew low. "It's in the middle of a moor, and freezing cold. Bring a bikini if you want to freeze your ass off."

I huffed, stalking into my bedroom. "Maybe if I do have witch magic, I could freeze *your* ass off."

4

"So when you said *hall*, you meant *Dracula's castle?*" I remarked, leaning forward to stare out the car window at the squat, blocky building sat atop the hill. We'd driven through scrolling iron gates with BLAKE HALL spelled out in cursive letters along the arch, and dark woods enclosed the path we drove on in complete and eerie silence[1]. "Ooh!" I spun to face Dean, my eyes wide with newfound excitement. "Tell me there are *bats*."

"There are no bats," he replied in the same annoyed growl he'd used for the past two hours.

"Awww," I complained, slumping in my seat. "But they're so squishy and cute. I've always wanted a batty friend."

Dean laughed derisively. "There are vampires, one of which might be old enough to have a bat form."

I gasped, gripping his arm hard enough to bruise. "Please don't be fucking with me. Please be telling the truth. You wouldn't hurt me like this, would you, Sexy Sir?"

He smirked, as he did every time I called him that, which I kept doing because he liked it. "If you want my advice, you'll stay far away from him. He's dangerous and unbalanced."

I made a squeak of excitement. "You're telling me there's a cute, squishy bat—"

"Who's a deadly, blood-driven vampire—"

"Who might be my insanity soul mate?" I sighed wistfully out the window as gravel crunched beneath our tyres, the hall rising up above us in two storeys of dark, foreboding stone and windows I hoped would glow yellow at night like a Halloween illustration. There was even a tower.

Dean said nothing, but he was broody enough that I glanced at him. His knuckles were white on the steering wheel, his handsome face like cut stone.

"What?" Realisation hit. "Aww, don't get jealous, Deanny. I'll still love you every bit as much if I make new friends."

He rolled his eyes, something he did a lot. Or maybe just a lot around me. But I had a sneaking suspicion that he liked me teasing him.

"Hmm," I murmured, contemplative as he parked in front of a tall, dark wood door with ancient bronze knockers[2]. "Do I get more than one?"

"What?" he replied, ripping the keys from the ignition.

"More than one mate? You seem awfully wound up, Sexy Sir." I reached across to squeeze his shoulder, fondling the strength there in the guise of a massage. "Are you worried I'll have more mates?"

His whiskey eyes met mine in a glare. "You *could* have more, and I don't give a shit if you do."

"Liar," I argued, gliding my hand up to his neck and pulling him towards me. I meant to kiss him quickly, chastely, like a good girl, but the second our lips met, Dean snarled and grabbed my waist, kissing me with fierce, demanding need. I gasped into his mouth as the seatbelt yanked me away from him—and moaned, turning into a puddle of lustful goo as he slashed through the thick material with sharp claws and dragged me onto his lap, his tongue forcing mine into submission.

The keys got carelessly thrown onto the dashboard as he ground me down into his trouser-clad cock, leaving delicious bruises all across my hips.

"I knew you liked me," I said victoriously, gasping for air before I greedily sought out his tongue again. Every glide and flick made me wonder how his mouth would feel on certain other, throbbing parts. I couldn't hold back a groan, sinking my fingers into his silver hair and gripping hard, taking control of the kiss—

For exactly three seconds, until Dean's hand wrapped around my throat and tilted my head, allowing him to slant his mouth over mine and completely and utterly ravage my mouth. There was no other way to describe it than Dean was brutally fucking my mouth with his tongue, and I went cold all over, writhing faster against his hardness as my body begged to be fucked, too.

"It's a very bad idea to tempt me, Miss Falcon," he rumbled, sending shivers down my spine as he dragged a sharp tooth across my cheek and down my throat. "You won't be able to handle everything I'll demand from you."

"Give me everything," I replied breathily, tugging hard on his hair to bring his mouth back to mine, and reaching between us to squeeze his bulge with my other hand. "If I break," I shrugged, "at least I had fun."

Dean paused, staring deep into my eyes, and I swooned at the desire churning in his whiskey gaze. "There is something very wrong with you," he said, but low and husky, like it was a good thing.

"You're just getting that *now?*" I asked, stealing another kiss, this one forceful and wicked from the start.

I jumped at the feel of hot hands at my waistband, and groaned into Dean's mouth as he flicked the button of my jeans open, yanking down the zip. "Here?" I gasped, staring out the car windows at the gothic hall I was meant to be imprisoned in —trained in—whatever. If I had my way, the only thing that would happen inside those walls would be sex and murder, and more sex and more murder. Maybe both at the same time... My pussy turned molten at the thought. I'd always wanted to fuck someone in a pool of my enemies' blood, but people tended to look terrified when you suggested things like that. Wimps.

"People will see," I pointed out, my mouth falling open as Dean sucked a sensitive spot on my neck, and then found my weakest point: the hollow of my throat. My toes curled inside my shoes and I rode his lap harder, grabbing his back to bring him as close as possible. The friction was delicious, but nowhere near enough.

"Good," Dean growled, dragging my vest out from my jeans' waistband and ripping it over my head, my bra following immediately after.

"Ohhh," I said, grinning. "You're an exhibitionist?"

"No," he replied. "I just don't care who sees me owning my little slut."

My pussy *ached*, a whimper slipping free at his tone, at that name. And he heard it.

A wolfish[3] grin creased his face, baring sharp white teeth. "You really are a dirty girl if you like being called a slut."

"I wouldn't say I *liked* it," I protested, but far too weakly, and writhing against him undermined my words a touch. Just a hair. A *smidge*. Fuck, this felt too good to think straight, especially when his fingers found my nipples, tugging on them to bring me flush to his chest.

"Don't lie to me. Your pupils are dilated, your breathing is erratic, and you forget I'm a wolf." He dipped his face to my ear, catching the lobe between his teeth.

"*Ohholyfuck.*"

"I can smell your arousal," he said, with a quiet laugh that made my eyes roll back. "I know how much you love it."

"Fine, I like it. Bite me."

"With fucking pleasure," he replied, as if I meant it seriously, and I froze, hot all over, at the feeling of sharp canines tracing the column of my throat to where it met my shoulder. "Here would look nice, right where everyone can see."

"I'll wear a scarf," I breathed. Was I trembling? I was pretty sure I was trembling.

"You wouldn't dare." His teeth pressed deep enough for me to feel them but not deep enough to pierce.

"I would," I shot back, twisting my fingers in his hair.

In return he tweaked my nipple, and I arched against him with a ragged gasp. I'd had foreplay before but this ... holy shit, this was something else. "Then I'd have to punish you for disobeying me," he warned.

"How?" I rasped, sinking my teeth into my bottom lip as he tugged on my other nipple, a line of electric sensation shooting to my clit when he rolled it between his hot fingers.

"Hmmm," he mused, swirling his tongue over the scratches he'd left on my throat. "I could spank this ass until it was red and raw." He grabbed my backside hard, digging his fingers into my plump flesh. "But something tells me a girl like you would enjoy that. Would that make you wet, hmm, Rebel?"

"*This* is making me wet," I breathed, feverish with need. Any longer and I was going to break.

His laugh was unexpected and pleased. "Am I torturing you, babygirl?"

Oh, I liked *that* name. "Yes," I whined.

"Good," he replied, hard as iron.

I squirmed, my clit so swollen that a single swipe of my finger would make me come. But the fabric between us was making that a little fucking difficult, and I was impatient and surly about it. Though I couldn't deny I loved hearing him talk.

"Maybe that's how I'll punish you, then," he laughed. "Ruin all your orgasms."

"Don't you fucking dare," I warned, deadly serious as I wrenched back to give him a threatening glare. "I'll cut your innards out and wear them as jewellery. I'll skin your balls and make them into a purse. I'll—"

"Fuck," he rasped, his eyes seeming to glow. Was this ... was my threatening him with gory murder turning him on? I meant to tease him about that, but I was too distracted by him shoving my jeans down with impatient hands, leaving them hooked around my ankles as he freed his own cock with agitated fingers. He didn't even bother to take his trousers off; he only tugged his balls free, grabbed my hips, and slammed me down at the same time he surged up.

"Mine," he snarled viciously, setting a punishing pace and making the whole car rock and creak around us. I tried to laugh at that, but a moan swallowed the sound as he filled me over and over, not giving me time to adjust to his size, just taking what he wanted from me. It was so fucking hot, I was going to die. "This is my fucking pussy."

I honestly didn't care what he said in that moment; I just grabbed his shoulders and held on for dear life as he pounded up into me, the wet sound of him fucking me sexy as hell.

"My hot, sweet little pussy," he went on, panting for breath. One hand left bruises on my hip while the other gripped my hair and dragged my mouth to his for a scorching, messy kiss that had me throbbing around him. "Fuck, Rebel," he grunted, all the muscles straining in his neck. "You feel so good, babygirl."

I kinda loved all the names he called me, and I would have melted at the praise if I wasn't busy being struck by orgasmic lightning.

The deep groan in his throat was the sexiest thing I'd ever heard, and I clung to him harder, digging my fingernails into his shoulders as I slammed my hips down to meet his; so, so fucking close.

"God, yes," he growled, dipping his head to suck my breast, teeth hard on my nipple. "You're so tight now," he said between sucks. "I bet this pussy's about to come for me, isn't it?"

Words were beyond me now; I just nodded fast and held on tight as his cock drove in and out. Everything disappeared—the wind howling outside, the ominous hall waiting to swallow me, the car squeaking and rocking furiously as we crashed together, as inevitable as waves breaking against the rocks.

I slid a hand between us and frantically circled my clit, my body locked tighter, tighter—

"Fucckkkkwow," I laughed as my climax hit, so powerful that I jolted and shook against him. My pussy locked tight around his cock as he kept fucking me, dragging out every bit of pleasure until I was as limp as a doll against his chest.

"That's it," he groaned, fingers pressed deep into my ass cheeks now. "Oh, fuck—"

I smiled as he came apart beneath me, crushing me to his body and sinking his teeth into the juncture of my neck and shoulder, making my inner walls clamp down around him once more. Pleasure washed over me in an endless wave until I was thoroughly dazed and beyond satisfied. I saw no need to move from this car for the next hour.

Or ever.

When he stopped throbbing inside me, Dean's tongue swept along my shoulder before he carefully removed his sharp teeth, lifting me off his cock. I whined, refusing to let go of him, and he laughed softly, settling me against his chest as we breathed long and deep, my head all floaty and soft.

Calloused fingers trailed up my back in a soft caress that made me snuggle closer, a smile tugging at my lips.

"This is not how I expected today to go," Dean admitted with a laugh, sounding less growly. He ran his fingers through my hair, gentle on the tangles, until he could cup the back of my head. My eyes rolled back, a more profound pleasure working through my body. No—deeper than my body. Through the mate bond? "But I can't say I have any complaints. We'd better go inside soon, though."

"Nnh," I replied eloquently.

His laugh warmed me from the inside out, and so did the soft kiss he placed on my bite. It should have stung, but all I felt was bliss and a not-unwelcome druggedness. "Well, you did say you didn't care if I broke you. You should have heeded my warning, Miss Falcon."

I just snuggled deeper into him, very happy with myself.

"Come on," he murmured a minute later, softly spanking my ass. "Get dressed. I'll show you around Blake Hall."

"Or we could fuck again," I countered, pouting when he gripped my waist and lifted me off him. My mouth went dry at the show of strength as he placed me in the seat beside him, not even breaking a sweat. "Fuck, you look so good like this," I said, reaching across to touch his messy hair, his eyes still glazed with lust and satisfaction and a smile curving his cheeks.

"Likewise, Rebel." His voice hardened. "Now get dressed. You're dripping all over my car."

I shrugged, unrepentant. "Just making sure you can never drive it again without thinking about me. Maybe I'll make sure my scent is everywhere," I threatened, propping my heels on the seat and spreading my pussy wide, trailing my fingertips through our combined fluids and fucking *delighted* at the savage snarl he let out. His hand snapped out to grab my wrist.

"I think," he rumbled, his voice like deep thunder, "you've pushed me enough for one day."

"Disagree, but fine."

His eyes softened with amusement, but the sharp edge remained. "Lick those fingers clean, and I'll consider you forgiven."

"I didn't actually apologise," I pointed out, but the command made me wet[4].

"Rebel," he warned, and I went cold and tingly, my mouth dry. I stuck my fingers inside it, making a show of sucking them, my own taste musky and sweet.

"Good girl," he praised, tucking his cock back inside his trousers[5] and zipping my favourite appendage into its cotton prison. "Now pull your jeans up and put this on." He threw my vest at me; I caught it out of the air just to spite him, and maybe to show off my fast reflexes. His eyes darkened, and I grinned, getting dressed like a perfectly respectable young lady[6].

"Lead the way, Sexy Sir," I said, and threw open my door, climbing out of the car.

He gave me an exasperated look; I batted my eyelashes

and followed him up the gravel driveway into the dark manor house.

I'd completely forgotten to ask why he got turned on at the thought of me carving out innards. Whoops. I'm sure it was probably nothing.

5

The bite below my neck was starting to sting, but I didn't let that dampen my enthusiasm as Dean led me up the wide steps and into a dark, gloomy foyer. I grinned, spinning in a circle and staring at everything: the tapestries hung on the walls depicting pastoral scenes, the heavily beaded lampshades, the dark tiled floor, the decaying flowers that mingled with the furniture wax and sweet alcohol scent in the air. It was deadly quiet in the entryway, the only motion a curtain on the landing above wafting in the wind of an open window, but I could hear distant voices in a different part of the building.

"Well, it's not as cute as my flat, but it'll do," I pronounced, tilting my head back to peer up at the frescoes on the ceiling. No blood and gore despite this being a hall for criminals and people with dangerous magic, just more perfectly normal scenes of ordinary people. I'd never seen anything that more clearly screamed 'nothing to see here, folks.' I snorted. "Where is everyone?"

"In the TV room," Dean replied, shutting the door

behind us with a thud. I twirled a strand of pink hair around my finger, beaming at him as he carried my bags.

"There's a TV room?" I gasped, staring up the stairs again. "Aren't you scared all us dangerous supernaturals are going to watch something scary and go psycho? Horror films have a bad influence on people, you know?" That was total bullshit, but I enjoyed teasing him.

Dean's rugged face split into a dangerous smile. "Why would we be scared, Miss Falcon? Anyone who steps out of line has to answer to me. And none have yet survived a fight against me[1]."

I shuddered, leaning against his side and rubbing like a cat. "Lucky me, having a big, bad alpha to stop all the dangerous people here hurting me."

The look he shot at me was amused. "Like you're not one of the most dangerous."

My lashes fluttered, my heart going all mushy and soft. "I like how well you know me, Sexy Sir."

His smack on my ass came as a shock, and my eyes flew wide at the crack of pain and heat. "Up the stairs. Now," he barked.

I bit my bottom lip and hurried to comply. Not because I was an avid rule follower, but because I was so turned on I forgot to push back against the command. I wanted him to bend me over the staircase bannister and take me again, wanted him to fuck me against every damn inch of this hall. But laughter rose up in the distance, muffled by walls and corridors, and my curiosity got the better of me.

"Wrong way, Miss Falcon," Dean called, all stern and in control. My nipples were hard again, my gut all squirmy with butterflies.

But I kept going the 'wrong' way, following the sound of

laughter and voices, interested to know who else occupied this hall for wayward witches, wolves, and vampires. I doubted I was in any danger—I was at the top of the food chain in any situation—but it'd be nice to make a few crazy friends. I'd always wanted someone to chat with about girly things, like how best to get bloodstains out of bubblegum pink dresses. And there was a subtle pull guiding me left, down the dark, wood-panelled corridor past paintings of dour women and proud men. I peered through the glass inset in each heavy door I passed, spotting a classroom-ish space I had no interest in, and two rooms that looked like counsellors offices. Near the end of the hall, past a room filled only with bean bags,[2] I found the television room Dean had mentioned.

"Rebel," the Sexy Sir in question growled in exasperation. "You're not due to meet everyone else until tomorrow. I'm taking you straight to your room to get settled in."

I spun and stuck my tongue out at him. "Too bad. Unless your plan involves you 'getting settled' into my pussy again, I'm not interested. I *am* interested in seeing what counts as a dangerous supernatural around here."

He only sighed, but I didn't miss the quiet growl laced through the sound. He wanted me again, there was no doubt about it, and a thrill ran down my spine.

The dark wood door was cracked partly open, allowing the voices—both full and real, and tinny and electronic—to filter out into the hall, and if I wasn't mistaken, someone was smoking in there. The scent of cigarettes was unmistakable —and yucky. I made a face as I pushed the door open with the toe of my boot, propping my hip against the doorway and grinning at the room full of seventeen people. Not a huge crop, and less than I'd been expecting.

"Hello ickle witchies, hungry vampies, and growly wolfies."

Immediately all eyes swung to me, and I grinned, giving an airy wave. I spotted lots of regular-looking folks[3], a couple huge, muscly men and women who had to be wolves, dark-haired, pale-skinned vampires with fangs poking free, and snotty-faced witches who took one look at me and scoffed. And a few decent witches, decked out in crystals and snarky T-shirts, who gazed at me with curiosity. Those I'd leave alive. The snooty bitches would suffer a sad, tragic, completely accidental murder if they spoke even one nasty word to me.

"Who the hell are you?" an elegant, red-haired woman asked, standing from her perch on the window seat[4] and flattening creases from her deep green dress as she frowned at me. My psycho-dar didn't go *pingpingping*, so I wasn't too worried about her, but it would have been stupid to underestimate any vampire. They moved super fast, were extra strong, and always hungry. I would make a tasty snack, but I'd prefer to keep my blood on the *inside* of my body.

"Depends which circle I move in," I replied with a smirk. I contemplated telling them my assassin name, but the last thing I needed was someone getting a bee in their snooty bonnet and telling the police where to find the most notorious hitlady this side of the Atlantic. "You little duckies can call me Rebel."

A rough hand closed around the back of my neck, and cool tingles rushed down my body, my smirk deepening as Dean's fingers dug in, a silent warning to be good.

The effect on the room's occupants was instantaneous. Backs straightened, gazes dropped to the floor, and sneers and snarls were wiped into neutral expressions. It was kind of hot how scary he was to all of them. And when I said *kind of* hot, I meant *holy fuck, take me right here, right now* hot.

"Everyone, meet your new neighbour," Dean said in his low, growly voice. "Rebel Falcon."

A low, snide laugh was the only reply, and I froze. "Does your family know you still use their name?" a sneering male voice asked, and my temper grated to shreds as a tall, heavily tattooed man a year older than me stepped out from a huddle of witches. The smirk on his face was every bit as sharp as the scythes tattooed on his biceps, his black eyes even darker than the ink on his throat, his hands, and his chest.

My blood ran cold, and then turned to pure ice, cold enough to burn. "What the fuck are *you* doing here?" I snarled, flattening my palms to my thighs where a flexible blade was sewn into my jeans. I'd gouge his eyes out, carve his heart out, slice his cock into teeny, tiny pieces—

Edison Bray just laughed, a sneer heavy in his voice. "I live here, Graves."

I winced, and hoped no one else knew the significance of that name. Hopefully they'd think it was a nickname. Unfortunately for me, the icy-haired prick stalking towards me with his tattooed hands shoved in the pockets of his black jeans was one of three people who knew I was Graves and killed people for a living[5]. "Go live somewhere else," I hissed, picking at the loose stitches on my jeans and freeing my throwing knife.

"Miss Falcon," Dean warned, but I was beyond warnings from super hot professor types now. I was breathing hard and fast, pain and murderous rage forming a tight knot behind my ribcage as I stared at Edison fucking Bray, looking every bit as smug and superior as the day he rejected me.

This bastard, with his black eyes and dangerous smirk, was my fated mate. And he made it very clear he'd rather shove his dick into a paper shredder than touch a dud like me. Again.

Well, jokes on you, asshole. Now I have crazy powerful magic that could level cities according to Dean.

"Why should *I* move?" Edison asked coolly, looking down his nose at me as he stopped in front of me. I tilted my head back[6] and bared my teeth, wishing I could call on some wolfieness and make them sharp and deadly. "I've lived here for nine months. You go find somewhere else to live, *Graves*."

Okay, that was *it*. How dare he sneer my name! The one good thing I had in my life, the career I'd built painstakingly for myself until I was amazing at it. I'd like to see *him* hunt and kill someone without leaving any evidence for the cops.

"I'm going to make all your innards outards," I hissed, and whipped my tiny blade up, opening a line of blood on his shoulder. Crimson blood spilled over the dark rose inked there, and my lady bits went all tight and tingly. *Not now, dammit, and definitely not* him.

He didn't want me, didn't want to even be in the same room as me, and I refused to let that hurt.[7]

"Again with the innards," Dean said under his breath, his big arms locking around me before I could do any worse damage to Edison Bray. But I grinned, big and unhinged, as Edison lifted a hand to the cut on his shoulder, the blood bright red on the pads of his fingers. He lifted his head slowly, his black eyes promising murder. *Bring it, bitch.* I had two years' worth of rage and heartache to work out, and I'd be happy to deal with that in a rational, well adjusted way: by beating the crap out of the person who hurt me. A stab here, a dismemberment there. I'd feel *much* better after that.

Dean's fingers gripped my wrist and squeezed so hard that I gasped, my little blade hitting the ground. No matter how hard I fought and struggled, my snarls sounding eerily wolf-like now I was out of control, I couldn't get my knife back.

"I'll finish stabbing you later," I threatened Edison as he crossed his arms over his chest and leant against a chair back, watching Dean haul me out of the television room with a smirk.

"I highly doubt that, but you can try," he taunted. To rub in that I was inferior and unworthy, he let bright green flames leap to his fingers and fluttered them in my direction, a reminder I'd never have magic, never live up to his perfect standards, never be a real witch.

On the outside I bared my teeth and planned his murder, but on the inside, all my carefully constructed walls of self confidence and badassery came crashing down around me. By the time Dean had hauled me across Blake Hall and opened a dark door, thrusting me inside, I was the broken little girl who would always be the shame of her witch family, who'd never be worthy of perfect Edison Bray.

But what had perfect Edison Bray done to get himself sent to Blake Hall, home of rejects and criminals?

"You just had to cause trouble on day one, didn't you?" Dean was ranting, manhandling me across a thick rug in my new room and depositing me on the bed. I half hoped he'd put me across his knee and spank me for my disobedience, just for something to cling to, something else to feel other than this gaping chasm about to swallow me. But he stepped away the instant he let go, disapproval and—oh, fuck—disappointment on his lined, stubbled face.

"He's my—" I began, but he cut me off.

"I don't give a shit, Rebel. You don't fight your neighbours, understood?"

"Inmates, more like," I muttered, earning a sharper flash of anger. But this time I wasn't teasing him for fun, and I got no satisfaction from it. I wanted ... fuck, I wanted him to take me in his arms and give me a big bear hug.[8]

"I'm locking you in your room overnight," Dean growled, his mouth in a thin line as he glared at me. "Maybe all tomorrow too, if you're still misbehaving. Someone will bring you food, but otherwise—"

"I'm grounded?" I finished bitterly.

"Yes," he agreed firmly. "Take the time to think about what you did wrong, and what you're *not* going to do next time."

"This is bullshit, Dean," I sighed.

His whiskey eyes flashed. "You can't go around stabbing people, Rebel."

"I didn't even stab him," I grumbled under my breath. "It was a tiny slice, hardly worth all this overreaction."

"If you don't fix your attitude, you'll never prove that you're safe to release into supernatural society," he warned. "And you'll be here forever. Or you'll be shipped to even worse places."

I laughed, choking on the sourness of that future.

"I'll be back tomorrow to unlock your door," he said, and slammed it shut before I could jump up and plead for mercy.

"Please," I whined, hoping he was standing on the other side, listening.

But he never replied. And I was left alone in my new room to think about my actions.

Not even seeing my surroundings, I threw myself onto the plush, four-poster bed and curled up with my knees to my chest, wishing I could stop reliving that day two years ago.

I should have killed Edison. He'd probably have killed *me*, just to rid himself of the shame of being the fated mate of a magic-less witch, a failure, a reject.

6

wo years ago

YOU KNOW that scene in the second *Harry Potter* book,[1] where the Dursleys tell Harry to go up to his room and pretend he doesn't exist? That was my life. Every. Single. Day.

The ballroom at Falcon Manor was set up like a wedding reception, with big circular tables overflowing with cream silk and rose gold cutlery, vats of mashed potatoes and platters of suckling pig on each one, stinking the room until it was a mess of roast meat, competing perfumes, and fresh roses and lilies. Weren't lilies supposed to be the flower of death? Maybe I should steal one and wear it in my hair, make it my symbol, a silent warning that I was more than what they saw—or rather overlooked and preferred to not see. I was sat at the furthest table, in the back where the real witches could pretend not to see me.

I was more than a failure of a witch, the only dud in the

Falcon witch line, the black sheep and secret shame of a family powerful enough to take over the world. And the Falcons *had* taken over the world—I had cousins who advised kings and queens, an aunt who sat in the House of Lords in disguise, and a whole gamut of family members who owned—or controlled—businesses that made billions of pounds on a yearly basis. If the Falcons wanted something to happen, they had more than enough power and influence to make it happen, and that was without adding magic into the mix. But I was a badass assassin; I was better.

I pushed cold carrots around my plate as the uncle on my left leant a little too close for my liking, talking to the random family member on my right[2] and casting a glance down my bodice. See this is why I hated wearing the shit my family picked out for me—or rather the army of maids, ladies, and tailors picked out for me. They were always figure hugging, and bosom-enhancing, and drew too much attention. And since I was never seated at tables with the other witch lines my powerful aunt was entertaining tonight, the only people who got to benefit from that enhanced bosom were my cousins and uncles.

I gritted my teeth as Uncle Niall enthusiastically replied to Random John[3], brushing up against my shoulder. A hundred ways of killing him flashed through my mind. I could take the knife pinned at my garter and jam it up into his throat. Blood would splash everywhere, covering the suckling pig, my limp carrots, and colouring the champagne bubbling away in glasses between us. It would also soak into my pale gown, and splatter my heinous bosom, which would be an avant garde look I knew I could pull off. Sadly, there'd be screaming and running and accusatory looks. And probably a squad car towing me away at the end of the night. Again. Pass.

I could unpick the heavy trimming from the edge of my bodice and use it to strangle him, but some killjoy would probably drag me away before I could finish the job.

Or I could open my clutch bag and pretend to take out a mirror to check my make up—and slip a dissolvable pill of poison into his drink. No one would ever believe it was me.

I was about to reach for my bag when Aunt Denise stood from the big table where the most powerful of the Falcon family were seated and tapped her fork against her champagne glass. A hush fell over the huge room, and the string quartet playing quietly in the corner cut out, leaving a sudden silence that exposed the argument going on beyond the row of french windows, Sue and Steve arguing[4] on the patio.

"Nobody gives a shit about your peach pie, Susan," Steve shouted, oblivious to the fact we could all hear every word. I pressed a smile into the corner of my mouth, leaning back in my chair and watching everyone shuffle uncomfortably. "Everyone prefers Viola's apple crumble anyway, so I don't know why you bother making it every damn week."

"You're only saying that because you want to fuck Viola!" Sue screeched, and I chuckled under my breath. Gasps and low murmurs echoed from the high, polished ceiling.

"To be fair," John[5] said, leaning in to talk around me to my uncle, "everyone would fuck Viola given half a chance."

"Isn't Viola your cousin?" I cut in dryly, blinking with innocent naivety when both their glares narrowed on me. *I'm just a sweet seventeen-year-old girl, and I can't possibly fathom that a man would screw his cousin.*

They ignored me, which was par for the course. Even these slimy pricks had a spark of magic, unlike me. In the witch lines, magic was might, and that was especially true of the Falcon witches. The witches with the most magic sat at the high table, and the ones with specks sat here on the fringes, forgotten and looked down on. I was lucky to get an invite at all, but I knew that was only because my absence would encourage gossip, and Aunt Denise *haaaaated* gossip.

I tuned out everything Denise said, only perking up when she said the dancing was about to start. Sometimes I thought we lived in a period novel, with all these balls and dancing and suitors and the marriage obsession. I needed to get out of this life, or I'd end up married to John[6]. Aunt Denise would probably hope to breed some power into me, as disgusting as that was.

But at least the dancing meant I could leave this table, hoist my bodice up, and blend into the shadows along the back wall. If I was lucky, the patio would be empty now Sue and Steve had stopped yelling at each other. I drained my glass of champagne, subtly burping the bubbles out instead of loudly belching them[7], and readjusted my dress as I skirted the edge of the ballroom in the direction of the patio.

The band struck up a louder song, strings filling the air alongside chatter and flirting, but I ducked out the back door before the dance could begin. When I was little, I'd wistfully waited to be invited to dance—and waited, and waited, and waited, until I'd figured out no one was ever going to ask me. I hadn't had a *terrible* childhood. I'd grown up in a ritzy house, with all the food I could want, a comfy bed, and warm rooms, and showers that were always hot. That was more than some people had. But most importantly, I'd had Ana, my awesome big sister who took care of me when Mum died young. Ana was the one who killed the monsters under my bed, and read me stories at night, and helped me get dressed, and played hide and seek with me in the manor gardens.

When I lost Ana ... it became pretty fucking clear this

place wasn't my home, these people weren't my family, and I didn't belong here. But I was still here, waiting, hoping. Stupid.

I pushed open the glass door and stepped out into the night, relieved at the sting of cold wind as it cleared my head, sharpened my thoughts and—

And Steve was balls-deep in Sue a few feet away, fucking her against the wall to her mewling encouragement.

"Honestly, Sue," I huffed, shaking my head as they startled and threw a panicked glance my way. "Have some self respect."

Rolling my eyes, I turned and stalked back into the ballroom, sliding the glass shut behind myself. And halted as a trio of Bray witches stalked past, looking ready for a fight. I followed their line of sight and saw they were headed for three of my capricious, dickhead cousins, and a smirk curved my mouth.

"Where have they been hiding you, pretty blossom?" a male voice asked, and I raised an eyebrow as one of the Brays broke away from the pack, sauntering over. I let my eyes pour down his body, from the hint of ink peeking above his white dress shirt, to the cheekbones cut sharply into his face, the icy blonde faux-hawk flopping to one side of his head, and black eyes currently smoky with interest as he gave me a similar perusal.

I wondered if he saw my tattoos beneath the sheer sleeves of the dress, if my pink hair gave me away as a different breed of Falcon, like his tattoos and sharp intensity gave *him* away as 'other.' The Bray witches were as bad as the Falcons—judgy and pretentious and so fixated on purity that nothing else mattered. If he was inked and as dangerous as he looked, he was either so weak they didn't give a shit what he did ... or so powerful that he could get away with anything.

"Pretty blossom?" I replied, crossing my arms over my chest and giving him an unimpressed look. "That's the best you could come up with? Let me guess, it's because my hair's pink."

He waved a hand at his cronies, sending them on, his hands tucked in his pockets and his eyes intent. "Maybe it's because I'm going to pluck you out of this place and keep you for myself."

I snorted. "*That's* the line you're going with? Pathetic."

His eyes sparked, and he prowled closer, so near I could feel the heat radiating off him, and see the flecks of paler grey in his black eyes. Holy fuck, he was hot, and his aura screamed *I will murder anyone who even dares to look at you*, which was my type.

"What's your name?" he asked, all demanding and sexy. I stifled a shudder, and fought the urge to throw myself at him while I was at it.

"None of your business," I replied coyly, tapping his chest with a pink fingernail. "You don't need to know my name to have fun with me."

A smile split his face, making his dark eyes glow. "Good point. Follow me, and don't be obvious about it, Blossom."

"Me? Obvious?" I twirled a strand of hair around my finger and batted my lashes. "I wouldn't know how to be obvious if you paid me."

The Bray snorted. "Didn't know you were that kind of girl, Blossom."

"Hey!" I hissed as he disappeared into the crowd of dancing tuxedos and flaring skirts. I didn't fuck for money. "Bastard."

But I still wound my way around the ballroom and

slipped out the door after him, skipping down the hall and giggling as he grabbed my waist bruisingly tight and slammed me into the wall hard enough to topple the vase propped against it. I laughed as it crashed to the polished marble, shards exploding everywhere as I grabbed my new playmate's icy hair and hauled him to my mouth.

"You're so fucking hot," he growled against my lips, kissing me with a ferociousness that knocked our teeth together and drew blood from my lip. My heart soared, my clit equally invested in this fumble. When his teeth scraped down my jaw and nipped my throat, I went pliant and loose, hot all over.

"Less talking, more fucking my brains out," I gasped, pawing at his black jacket until it slid off his shoulders, exposing so much mouthwatering ink beneath his white, almost-transparent shirt.

His laugh moved straight to my pussy, dragging a spasm from my aching walls. "I like the way you think, Blossom," he said, husky with desire as he bundled my skirts around my waist. Magic made me jump as it tingled over my skin, an unfamiliar brush of lightning, and the bastard laughed as my underwear disintegrated.

"Skittish thing, aren't you?"

"Shut up," I hissed, and hauled his vicious mouth back to mine, kissing him fiercely as he fumbled at his zip. I didn't care that we could still hear the music of the ball, or that voices floated down the corridors, or that a window was open nearby to let cold night air in—and the sounds of our voices out. None of that mattered when the tip of his cock slid over my clit in teasing circles that had me writhing against him, my leg hooked around his waist. I didn't care about being seen or getting caught as we kissed and groaned and he sank to the hilt inside me. My eyes flew wide at the sudden fullness, the stretch.

"Fuck, that pussy's good," he groaned, his face pressed to my throat and teeth skimming my sensitive spots as he withdrew from my pussy and slammed back in until our hips met. I clenched and throbbed around him as he held there, a smug laugh rumbling his chest. "How long until you come, Blossom? Three strokes? Two?"

I hated the fucker for being right, and internally growled at myself for getting so turned on that his words nearly tipped me over the edge. "If you can't handle it," I panted, "I can find a man with better stamina."

He drew back so suddenly, grabbing my throat and putting pressure on the sides. My tongue lolled out of my mouth and I panted, so aroused I ached, writhing to get him deeper as he kept still inside me. "Careful how you taunt me."

"Or what?" I gasped, half praying he'd threaten me. Call me fucked up, but there was nothing as sexy as a dangerous man. And besides, if he really *did* try to hurt me, I'd slit his throat and leave his body cold on the ground, his cock still hanging out.

But this man was so hot, and so dark with that glint in his eyes, and his body was too beautiful to leave in a bloody heap.

"Or," he growled, bringing his face so close to mine that I went cross-eyed trying to focus on him, "I'll make you come so many times you'll be sobbing by the time I'm done. You'll beg me to stop touching your clit," he warned, holding me against the wall with his hips, his cock buried in my throbbing heat. "And I'll ignore you, and keep dragging orgasm after orgasm from you." He laughed, a cruel sound that had me panting, arching up into the hand around my throat. "I doubt you'd be able to think or stand by the end. I'll leave you here, dazed and dumb, for anyone else who might come along."

Okay, that definitely should not have aroused me.[8]

"Dirty girl," he laughed, feeling how much I loved his threats. He squeezed my throat and then let go, slapping my bare thigh before he shoved it down and withdrew. He handled me like a doll, and my mouth filled with saliva, my heart pumping fast as he spun me and shoved me face-first into the wall, dragging my skirts up as he sank back inside and set a punishing pace. "I bet you'd love it if someone found us here like this."

"Yes," I gasped, scratching the wallpaper off the wall as his cock ruined me. How he expected me to stand up, I had no idea.

His hand came down on my ass and I made a choked sound of surprise, my head shooting up at the bright pain and then the deep heat that moved through my cheek. "Shame I didn't bring my friends to share you, hmm?"

"Fuck," I choked out, so fucking close now. My toes curled inside my shoes as he fucked me deep.

"No," he snarled, his hips bruising my ass with his intensity. "I don't want to share you. You're all mine, pretty blossom. You're my—shit," he breathed, thrusting all the way inside and throbbing inside me, making me explode around him as he came, too.

Damn, it was … damn.

My breath came hard and slow, my eyelids heavy over my eyes even though we were in the middle of a corridor and my dress was shoved up to expose my pussy and ass—and his cock still buried deep inside me.

"Fuck, Blossom," he murmured, sliding out of me. "You're my mate."

"What?" I gasped—laughed.

I shook my head, shoving my dress back down and turning to face him. But what he said felt right, felt true, and I could sense it—the glow, the warmth in my belly. This hot as sin, dominant, tattooed man was my mate? I grinned, and he smirked back at me, his black eyes soft as he reached up to trace my cheek.

A whip-hard laugh made me flinch back, and my shoulders drew up as I recognised it. "What are you doing with *her*, Edison?" one of my fouler cousins asked. Sometimes I fantasised about pulling her brain out through her nostrils like the Egyptians used to. She deserved it, and quite frankly, she'd be a much nicer person with half her brain removed.

"Piss off, Antonella," the man who'd just fucked me against the wall spat, derision and scorn dripping from every part of him. He'd tucked his cock back in his pants, but it was pretty clear what we'd just done.

Wait. *Edison?*

My stomach plummeted, and I crossed my arms over my chest, taking a step back. Edison Bray. That was who he was. The fucking golden boy of the Bray family.

Shit.

How could the precious Edison Bray look like *this*? How could he be wicked and cruel and inked on every bit of exposed skin? My breath caught, panic spiralling through me. I tried to reach for Graves, my inner badass, but she slipped out of my grasp.

"You do know who she is?" Antonella asked, laughing as she came closer. She was a duplicate of Aunt Denise, right down to the flaxen hair pinned on her head, the navy blue power suit, and the sharp, amused glare. "She's the reject of our family, she's a *dud*."

I held my breath, waiting for the laughter, barely daring to hope that Edison would come to my defense. He was my mate. He'd felt it, and I'd felt the pull towards him, too. *More* than that, even. It might have been rough and hard, but him fucking me against the wall had made an unbreakable tether unfurl in my middle like a flower under sunlight. It wasn't just a pull; we were fully *bonded*, and I had to hope he'd take my side, keep me close, and maybe—hopefully—kill Antonella for sneering at me.

"A dud," Edison repeated, giving me an inscrutable look. I lifted my chin high and challenged him with a glare. I had nothing to be ashamed of; it wasn't my fault I didn't have magic. Words I repeated to myself daily, even if I didn't quite believe them. Ever since Ana's death, everyone else's words had sunk a little deeper into my psyche.

"Not a drop of magic," Antonella confirmed, sounding beyond pleased to ruin this for me.

I saw it the second Edison turned to me—the disappointment, the anger, the hatred—and I touched the knife hidden at my thigh for reassurance.

"You're a dud?" he asked, his lip curling back from his teeth.

"Better that than a snivelling, spineless bitch," I fired back with a sneer at Antonella. I took a wild hit at him and added, "And a coward."

I knew it was disgust that made him look at me like that, but maybe it was fear of what people would say if they found out he had a dud for a mate, too.

"Pathetic," I said with a cruel laugh.

"*I'm* pathetic?" he replied coolly, a pale eyebrow raised. "This coming from the failure of a witch?" The little smirk cut too deep for someone I'd just met. He meant *nothing* to me. But that hatred in his eyes ... it carved into my heart. I'd just had him inside me, could still feel the gentle brush of his finger on my cheek as he gazed at me with softness. He laughed now, callous and heartbreaking and gave Antonella a grin. *Antonella.* "Thanks for telling me. I dodged a serious bullet with this thing."

Thing.

That word echoed in my head, the only thing I could hear. I swore for a second I saw regret flash in his black eyes, but that was just delusion.

"No problem," Antonella replied, smiling as she sauntered past, close enough to brush his arm. I saw red, anger and possessiveness exploding in me so fast I couldn't contain it.

I acted without thinking, whipping my knife free and ripping it across her throat, parting the thin skin there and smiling with satisfaction as blood poured free.

"Blossom," Edison gasped. "*No.*"

His arms banded around my middle, pulling me away as I moved to open more and more wounds on my hateful cousin. But it was too late for him to save her, and I laughed, a little broken, a little psycho.

"What have you done?" he demanded, setting me on my feet and spinning me to face him. "Do you have any idea what you've done?"

"Killed a constant thorn in my side?" I asked with a shrug, letting him see all the crazy shining through my eyes. "Careful, Edison, or I might kill you, too."

"I'd like to see you try, dud," he replied, magic sparking around his hands, spitting onto my skin and dragging gasps of pain from me. But that didn't deter me; I was too far gone to think clearly. "Why couldn't you be a normal witch?" he demanded.

I whipped my knife up and pricked his throat, and he

instantly let go. Panting hard, emotions whipping through me like a storm, I staggered back. I was leaving. I wasn't staying in this place a second longer. I couldn't. "Why couldn't you be a decent man?" I shot back, retreating step by step, unable to resist a smirk at the pool of blood spreading on the ground. Antonella deserved it. She'd tried to poison my mate against me. Had succeeded. "You might hate me, Thomas Edison—" I taunted, instinctively knowing it would tick him off.

"That's not my name," he growled, black eyes flashing with warning.

"—But I'm your mate," I finished with a grin, knowing I looked unhinged as it spread across my face. I didn't care. Didn't care about anything except getting out of here. I was done—I'd be Graves from now on, and only Graves.

Edison laughed. "I don't give a shit what you are. I don't want you. Why would I? I'm the most powerful heir to the Bray line. Why would I mate a dud?" He gave me a pitying look so much worse than his sneers. "Did you think we were going to live happily ever after?"

"I'm going to kill you," I hissed, backing up. "Not now. Not tomorrow. But someday, I'm going to kill you, Edison Bray."

"I look forward to it," he replied, and gave me a last smirk before sauntering down the corridor back to the ballroom.

Tears rolling down my cheeks, I fled to my bedroom, and threw my things into a bag with shaking hands, unable to hear anything except those four words on repeat.

I don't want you.

7

resent Day

I ALLOWED myself to wallow for a minute—fine, three hours—before I grabbed a tissue from the ornate wooden box at my bedside[1] and blew my nose, banishing thoughts of that bastard witch Edison Bray.

The tears on my face took two more tissues to dry, but I didn't feel any better or clearer-headed, or any other magical resolution crying was meant to bring me. I just felt nasally and pathetic. What I needed was a job, someone to sneak out of this hall to kill. But Dean was growly and pissed off enough, and the part of me that was still small and aching and desperate for affection didn't want him to be angrier at me.

Besides, the bed was comfy. Why bother moving?

I stretched out on top of the dark green covers, gazing up at the whorls of plaster on the ceiling. This whole room looked like something out of a museum or a stately home. I wouldn't have been surprised if Henry VIII hadn't lived here with one of his wives. Although the thought of them rutting away on the bed beneath me made my nose wrinkle. Ick.

I narrowed my eyes at the tall wardrobe opposite, and the chest of drawers beside it, wondering if some ancient Tudor couple had fucked there, too. Maybe even on the desk in front of the window, knocking off all the pots and pens.

"Dammit," I huffed, dragging a hand through my pink hair. "Now I'm just turning myself on. Stop thinking about Tudor people fucking. Or regular people fucking. Think about murder, a nice, gory, bloodsoaked murder."

A dreamy smile crossed my face as I thought of my last fun kill. Not Dicky, that boring douche. No, the job before that had been *much* more difficult—and fun—because my target fought back, and he was damn good at it too. He'd called me so many mean, belittling things I'd had to make him pay for, and I'd carved him into a beautiful work of art. I'd left a big love heart on his chest with 'Graves' above it and 'murder' beneath. On his back, I drew a unicorn with a massive cock, the tip dangling right above my target's buttcrack. It was both a hobby and a clever ploy to scare the shit out of people, and it worked. Even hitmen and hitladies —and hitfolks for the non-conforming rebels—kept their distance from me, as if crazy was a disease they could catch.

I'd been perfectly sane once, a regular, sweet, mind-mannered girl.[2] But then Kyle Ladislav happened.

My blood boiled and my insanity meter spiked at the thought of my sister's boyfriend, but before I could plummet into a murderous rage and take it out on my new bedroom, something scratched at my bedroom door.

"Kitty?" I asked hopefully, but thumbed a knife free of its sheath at my waist and slid off the bed, shaking all the tension from my muscles until I was ready to stab a bitch. If it was Edison Bray coming to fight me, I'd cut his dick off before he could even blink. He didn't deserve that dick after the way he'd fucked my brains out and then ripped out my heart.[3]

How many women had he been with since? The thought made my hands shake and my nostrils flare, even though I was a complete hypocrite who'd had super hot car sex that afternoon.

The scratching came again, followed by a thud against the door that made it rattle in its frame. I straightened, instantly on alert, but I tilted my head at the gravelly voice that crooned, "I can smell you in there, sugarplum. Your blood calls to me, and your soul sings to mine."

I held my knife casually at my side as I approached the door, propping my hip against the wall beside it. "Who the hell are you?"

"Calvin Woods," he rasped. "Everyone calls me Slasher."

I perked up instantly. "Slasher? Why that name?"

"It suits me. I need to lick you, taste you." He groaned, the sound muffled, and I blinked at the wet, slurping sounds.

"Are you ... licking the door?"

"I *need* you," he pleaded, his voice a rasp. "Please let me inside, cupcake."

"I thought I was sugarplum?" I remarked, cleaning my fingernails with my knife as a smile played at my lips.

"You're everything delicious and delectable that has ever existed," he replied in a gravelly rush. "You're a temptation and a lure. Why does your soul call to mine, bubblegum?"

I laughed at the name, thinking it fit my personality quite well. Slasher and Bubblegum. We could be a supervillain duo, murdering annoying doo-gooders and pretentious joggers.

Wait. I shook my head to clear the fantasy. My soul called to his? Like it did to Dean and that other fucker we wouldn't mention. "Are you my mate?" I asked with a laugh. How many did I have? Four? Five? Fifteen? I winced, scratching my head with my knife. I hoped it wasn't fifteen; three cocks I could manage, five if I got my hands involved, but where would I even put fifteen? Someone would feel left out, and that wasn't fair.

"Mate," Slasher breathed, the wet sounds stopping. He was quiet for so long that I thought he'd walked off, but then a rush of air moved down the hall outside like a whistle and a dark blur barraged into my new bedroom door, knocking the solid wood off its top hinge.

"Holy fuck," I breathed appreciatively at the destruction. And then gulped as Slasher blurred, instantly in front of me, his hands on my waist.

"Candyfloss," he groaned, staring down at me.

I blinked, and then blinked again. I'd guessed as much from his need to taste me, but he was a vampire, and a damn old one judging by his insane speed and strength. His crimson eyes lit up as he met my gaze, and his pale face split in an unhinged, fangy grin. Fuckkk, those teeth looked pointy and sharp.[4] His cheekbones were almost as sharp, cutting through his aquiline face and giving him a gaunt, aristocratic look that was only enhanced by his straight nose and severe jaw.

"You," he breathed, sounding so desperate, "smell good enough to eat."

"No eating," I warned, tapping him on the nose like he was the cute kitty I'd hoped he'd be. A scary hot, danger kitty more like. Luckily for me, I didn't run at the sight of danger. I threw myself at it, boobs first.

Slasher's eyes went big and pleading, irises the colour of red wine. "Ever?"

I sighed, pondering as I fell into his hypnotic eyes. "Mmm, maybe sometime. But not now." But I groaned when he ducked his head and an ice cold tongue lapped at my throat, a throb in my pussy answering every stroke over my neck. Should I have pushed him away? Probably. Was I going to? Hmmm, maybe in a minute, this felt fucking good.

And besides, I needed a distraction from wallowing in misery.

"How old are you?" I asked, gasping when his hands moved from my waist to cup my boobs through my shirt. It was the strangest sensation, like being caressed by a soft, pliant ice cube. My nipples hardened against his palms and I ground shamelessly against him, pouting when I didn't feel an erection.

Wasn't he turned on by this like I was?

Oh.

Wait.

He was a vampire ... and erections needed blood ... could he only get hard when he fed? Fuuck, that was sexy and I had no idea why.[5]

"Five hundred and two," he replied, licking my throat and groaning deep in his throat. The low, rattling sound made me clench, and I sank my hands into his long black hair.

I arched up as he nipped my throat in a tantalising path. "Well, I've always liked older men."

And I'd never been one to look a gift horse[6] in the mouth. If this vampire wanted to make love to the erogenous zone on my throat, I wasn't going to stop him. Coming to Blake Hall had to have perks, after all.

"Your skin tastes so good, lemondrop," Slasher groaned,

licking up to my jaw. "I want you."

"Fuck," I breathed, tightening my fingers in his hair and rubbing against him like a cat in heat. "Why does that make me so horny?"

"Let me bite you, pancake, and I'll satisfy your need."

I laughed, the names getting more ridiculous every time. Slasher pulled back, his expression tight with intensity and his red eyes gleaming with a sheen of madness I usually only saw in myself. I grinned suddenly, tightening my fingers in his hair until it had to hurt, and was rewarded by him twisting my nipples through my shirt.

"My mate," he said in a low, raspy voice, as if testing out the word. His throat bobbed as he swallowed, and his tongue darted out to wet his lips. "My delicious mate."

I reached inside myself and sought the new bond, beaming at the feel of it—like a live wire spitting electricity. "Do they call you Slasher because you like to cut people?" I asked, arching against him and licking his neck in a mirror of his earlier tasting.

"I'd never cut you, cinnamon bun," he vowed, utterly serious. His arms wrapped around my waist like bands of iron, and I melted at the sudden feeling of safety.

"But other people?" I pressed, sucking on the extra-slow pulse throbbing in his neck. "Would you cut them?"

"I'll try to be good," he swore. "I'll try to be good for you, my beautiful butternut, and I won't kill anyone, forever and ever. Just a few small cuts if someone really annoys me."

Aww, that was sweet. Totally unfounded, but sweet. "Don't be good; good's so dull." I sucked on that slow thud in his throat, scraping my teeth to see what he'd do.[7] He hissed, grabbing the backs of my thighs, and lifted me up in a blur. The lamp rattled on the table nearby as he slammed me against the wall, and I wrapped my legs around him, nestling my pussy over his cock. But I whined, wanting him hard and throbbing. "Can I tell you a secret, Slasher?"

"Oh fuck, please yes, cheesecake. Please tell me a secret." He ducked his head and licked furiously at my pounding pulse, starting to tremble.

"I'm not good, either," I whispered in his ear, carding my fingers through his long hair. "And I like slashing people, too."

He froze, his tongue against my throat, and then let out a long, gravelly moan. "You're the most perfect woman I've ever met, and I'll—"

"What the hell happened here?" an unfamiliar male voice demanded, and I gasped, twisting my head to see a tall, sandy-haired man in his forties frown at the door hanging half off its hinges. A name badge on his brown shirt proclaimed him to be Paulson. "Who did this?"

His eyes landed on me and narrowed, his mouth pressing flat, and—I stumbled back against the wall, not sure why I was suddenly off balance, just grappling for something to hold onto so I didn't fall onto my ass.

"Don't—" Thud. "Look—" Thud. "At—" Squelch. "My —" Crush. "Creme Brulee."

I laughed, my heart going all squishy and soft as Slasher caved Paulson's head in against the floorboards, his face so severe and gaunt. Did *I* look that crazy when I killed people? Slasher's eyes were narrowed and dark, his mouth tight and his nostrils flaring. But when he expelled a hard breath and lifted his hands, surveying his messy work, a smile kicked up the corners of his mouth and the tension left his eyes.

"I've been here less than a day, and already you men are killing for me," I said with a dreamy sigh. "I love this place."

"Men," Slasher repeated, unfolding to his feet so fast I missed the movement.

"I have other mates," I told him, and quelled his explosion of rage by adding, "but none are as bloodthirsty as you. Or as deranged as me."

His red eyes went all soft and puppy-like. "I suppose I could share you sometimes. But I get to keep you to myself, too."

"Deal," I agreed. Things were definitely looking up at Blake Hall; I had a dominant alpha and a bloody vampire who were both obsessed with me.[8]

A huge, manic grin overtook Slasher's sharp-planed face as he slid his fingers through the blood and brain matter splashed across my floor.[9] I watched with confusion as he rose to his feet and approached the wall where he'd sucked my throat, and then wrote SLASHER HEARTS PUDDING.

"You do know my name's Rebel?" I drawled to cover up the fact that my throat was thick and I was tearing up. He was so sweet, and cute, and covered in blood.

"The most delicious rebel pudding ever," he replied, as if that made any sense.

I laughed as he cupped my face with his bloody hands and laid the softest kiss on my lips. After his intense throat licking, it was a surprise, and I smiled, wrapping my arms around his neck and shivering at his coldness pressed to my front.

"I'll kill all your enemies," he murmured against my lips, his red eyes flashing. "And that's a promise, my beautiful panna cotta."

"I like you," I replied, kissing his cheek. "You're nice."

Yes, Blake Hall was definitely looking up, and I was excited to see what tomorrow would bring.

At least until tomorrow struck, and I realised everything wasn't all romantic murders and hot kisses. But that was a problem for tomorrow.

8

"This is meannn," I complained the next morning, scowling at Dean's handsome, rugged face, the scent of his aftershave teasing me from all the way across his desk. "It was one measly little body, and I didn't even kill the guy."

Dean Garrick, the sexiest of sirs to ever exist, wasn't moved by my complaining. If anything, his glare darkened, mouth pressing into an even thinner line. If he was thinking of the way he'd fucked me in his car yesterday, he certainly didn't show it, and I pouted, crossing my arms over my chest. The hard chair I sat in before his desk dug into my shoulder blades, adding insult to injury.

"You caused trouble within minutes of arriving, Miss Falcon," he growled, so much alphaness in his words that a shudder rippled through me. My nipples stood to attention, begging for his calloused hands. "And then hours later, we discovered an advisor murdered in your room."

"Yeah, but it wasn't *me*," I muttered, scratching my initials into the chair arm. "Why would I want to kill an advisor?"

"It's only because there's no possible way you *could* have killed Paulson that we're not kicking you out and sending you straight to prison."

My mouth dropped open in outrage, and I sat straighter in my seat, the fog of his sexy scent and his growl clearing in an instant. "*Excuse* me?"

Dean's whiskey eyes flashed with warning, and he gripped the armrests of his leather chair so hard his knuckles turned pale. I kinda wanted those hands on me, leaving pretty bruises on my hips, but I shook my head to dislodge the fantasy. Now was not the time or place; he'd been mean and then insulted me. He didn't deserve my pussy. "You can't believe we'd set you free when we found someone murdered in your room," he rumbled, his low voice drowning out the sounds of residents traipsing down the corridor outside.

"Not that bit," I huffed, waving a dismissive hand and scowling at his rugged face. "What do you mean I couldn't *possibly* have killed him?"

Dean's lips curved up at the edges, indulgent and amused. "He was much taller than you, and too heavy for you to take down on your own."

I'd taken down much bigger men, but I pressed my lips into a scowl, my nostrils flaring. I'd show him, and he'd feel like a silly fool when he saw me kill someone even bigger than Paulson. But not now. I was already being punished for bad behaviour, and I'd been at Blake Hall for less than a day.

It was not looking like I'd be sent back to society as a good, innocent girl. Which was really screwing with my plans—I needed to get back to my life.

"I'm still not doing the stupid detention." I scowled deeply, kicking one of his desk legs. This office was every bit as lavish and ritzy as I'd expected, full of ornate wood and cherry furniture and rich velvet fabrics. He even had one of those green desk lamps fancy folks had in films, and I reached over and pulled the dangling gold cord, making a rich glow erupt from the glass.

Dean's rough hand closed around mine and tugged, turning the lamp off. He held my hand so hard it started to hurt, and my stomach got all squirmy.

"It's not a detention," he said, deep and chilling. "It's a chance to prove to your advisors that you're worthy of rehabilitation. That we shouldn't throw you into a jail cell."

"Ooh!" I leaned forward, flashing him a considerable amount of cleavage as my boobs spilled out of my pink dress. It had skulls and crossbones and little knives all over it, which was extra fun. Girly and murdery? Count me in. "If you put me in a cell, we could play jailor and cellmate. You could take advantage of me." I fluttered my eyelashes, and watched his expression darken with reprimanding. "Maybe I'd have to suck your cock to earn a shower. Would you like that, Sexy Sir?"

"Rebel," he warned, gripping the arm rests of his chair so hard the wood cracked. I grinned, bouncing in my seat. "Would you *please* take this seriously? If you mess up these trials and prove unworthy, you'll be sent to jail for being a threat to paranormalkind, and your power will be stripped. You'll never get parole, or a hearing, you'll be left to rot."

"That sounds boring," I huffed, crossing my arms again and using them to push up my boobs, smirking when Dean's gaze glued to them before he growled and looked away. "I'd rather just stay here."

Not to mention I'd killed enough criminals that prison wouldn't end so well for me this time around. I might have been a total badass and the best hitlady to ever, ever exist, but I could only fight so many enemies at once. If I was outnumbered, I was dead. Juvie was one thing, but adult prison? Pass.

Seriousness came crashing down around me and I huffed a sigh, leaning back in the uncomfortable chair. "Fii-ine," I relented. "I'll do the stupid trials. What are they?"

"You say that like you have a choice," Dean muttered, but he grabbed a pen from the tidy pot on his desk and scrawled something on a piece of paper in my file. It was already chunky and full of paper, and curiosity burned at what it said about me. That I was the best knife thrower in the district? That my family were all a teensy bit scared of me? That I'd never been convicted for Antonella's death, but I'd been locked up for what I'd done to my sister's murderer. I bet every assessment from the psych at juvie was in there, and I tried not to wince. She hadn't liked me very much. "But I'm glad you'll cooperate. Your first task is tonight. You'll go out with the six others taking the trials and survive a night in the whimpering woods."

"Ooh," I breathed, my eyes lighting up. "Why are they whimpering? Do the trees cry? Do they talk like the grandmother tree thingy in *Pocahontas*?"

Dean fixed a flat stare on me, not responding to my excitement as he wrote a few more sentences before saying, "It's called the whimpering woods because most people come out crying." With a cruel smile he added, "If they come out at all."

My stomach twisted into a knot, my excitement popping like a balloon. That didn't sound good. Not good at all.

9

My first magic lesson went *so* well. I'd been given some one-on-one time with Vivian, the magic guidance counsellor at Blake Hall, a hippie woman in her forties with flowing blonde hair and a million beads dangling around her neck in a rainbow of colours. She was soooo pretty, but extremely dull, and the only bit of magic she managed to coax from me in our one hour session was the time I got bored and sang the entire 'Bohemian Rhapsody,' from start to finish. She ended with recommending me to Kris, Blake Hall's resident psychiatrist.

I wished Kris the best in assessing me, diagnosing me, and attempting to fix every glorious bit of madness in my head. Many had tried, and none had succeeded. But hey, it would give him something to do for the next few weeks. Months. However long I was stuck here.

At least Blake Hall didn't have timed showers, or people who'd shiv me on the way to and from my room every morning. And I didn't have to do laundry. I *hated* laundry. Sheets were like tribbles in *Star Trek*; I'd just get rid of one and a dozen more would multiply into existence. The moral of the story was it could always be worse; it could be prison.

"Remember, if you fail this, you're going to jail," I said under my breath as I lagged behind the seven other inmates —sorry, *residents*—following Dean down the sloping garden at the back of Blake Hall. The sun had set hours ago, making the whole place even more gothic and creepy, and moonlight silvered everything until the trees ahead of us were ghostly and ominous.

I'd always liked the nighttime; it was way easier to cover up a murder at night. But knowing my only task was to survive a whole night in this place made fear skitter down my spine and my hand flick to my thigh where I'd holstered a knife. I'd brought twenty three blades to Blake Hall with me—Dean either hadn't known they were there or didn't care—and I wished I'd worn them all tonight. I only had six. What if I needed seven? What if the woods were full of monsters that hungered for flesh? My flesh would be the tastiest of everyone's, I just knew it. The others sent to the woods for this trial were vampires and wolves—two vamps, five wolfies, all male—so of course the hungry monsters prowling the trees would want a bite of a witch-wolf dual-blood. The others were supermarket sushi, and I was an exceptionally rare caviar.[1]

"Your first test, as you know, is to spend a whole night in the whimpering woods," Dean said from the front of the group, pausing right before the towering wych elm trees. The shadows and moonlight made him look even more dangerous than normal, and I shuddered, wanting to press up against him and taste the slope of his jaw.

Wait, focus, Rebel. This could be important.

"You can use whatever magic you want, and any fangs, claws, and compulsion you have, too. The only rule is no harming each other, only the dark things that prowl the woods."

I shuddered again, this time from fear. Sexy Sir definitely had a way with words; I saw all the others exchange glances too. "Any questions?" he asked with a smirk that told me he was going to enjoy our suffering.

I scowled. Just because he was hot and dangerous and alpha didn't mean he had to be a psychopath about this.

"How will we know we've passed?" Brunel, a big, twenty-something wolf asked, his bald head resembling a hard boiled egg. I wondered if he was all yellow and fluffy inside like a yolk, and reached for my knife to crack him open and find out, but Dean spoke, snapping me out of the bloodlust.

"You'll know, because the sun will have risen. All you have to do is spend the night in there. Anyone who runs out before then forfeits their place at Blake Hall."

"Fuck," one of the other wolves muttered, this one a rangy bastard with lank black hair the others had called Vom. I assumed it was short for Vomit, a lovely name. "Then we'll be like the Discard Society."

"The what now?" I asked, frowning.

The third wolf—Frank, brunette and nondescript in every way except for a goatee that seemed to have died on his face—snorted, dismissive. "They're dead and gone. In the eighties, a group of paranormals who were kicked out of Blake Hall banded together and tried to kill everyone."

My eyes went wide. Woah, that sounded fun.

"So all we have to do is stay in there until it's light?" one of the vampires scoffed, Dauntley or something like that. He was nowhere near as pretty as my Slasher, more pustule-y and craggy, with blonde-ish hair and an old jacket severely in need of repair. Or being sent to its final resting place in the rubbish bin.

"Won't you go *poof?*" I asked with keen interest, peering at the vampires—the craggy one and his friend who looked like every teenager's wet dream with his sharp cheekbones and floppy brown hair. He must have been in a boy band. Must have been. Who cared if he could sing; those cheekbones qualified him.

Boyband snorted, looking down his nose at me. Okay, his cheekbones were less appealing now. I crossed my arms over my chest and scowled. "Not with these," he replied, and lifted a chain from his chest to show the vial pendant hanging from it.

"Ohhh, you've got those fancy witch potion things. Nice." I nodded, ignoring Dean's exasperated glare.

"You'll each go your separate ways," he growled, looking straight at Boyband. "No colluding."

Why did I think he made that rule up on the spot? I beamed, twirling a strand of hair around my finger. "Yes, sir," I said, sultry and low, and my stomach fluttered with butterflies at his low warning growl.

"In," he rumbled. "All of you. I'll be back at dawn to check on you."

"What's in there?" I asked, approaching my alpha mate as the others picked a direction and walked into the woods.

"Things that will try to eat you," he replied with a wicked smile. "Things that will skin your body and eat your bones."

My eyes widened. "You're not serious."

"Maybe, maybe not," he replied, and brought his hand cracking down on my ass. I jumped, yelping at the rough sting. "Get moving, Miss Falcon, or I'll throw you over my shoulder and carry you in myself."

I brushed up against him, licking his jaw like I'd wanted

to do earlier. The rough scrape of his stubble against my tongue was delicious.

"Alright, that's it," he growled, and I shrieked as I was suddenly airborne, my chest slamming into his back as he set off with fast, bouncing steps. "Dean, put me down!" I complained, wriggling in his hold and shouting as he spanked me hard again.

"Do you always have to be difficult?" he muttered, setting me on my feet so quickly that dizziness flared in my head and I tipped forward. His hands caught me, so big they spanned my shoulders, and I swooned.

"You love it," I laughed. But I saw that he'd set me down beyond the tree line, and unease curdled my stomach, wiping the smile off my face. "How is this supposed to prove I'll be a good paranormal in the future? Something could eat me!"

Dean ducked his head to kiss my cheekbone. "You'll be fine. You're a smart girl, Rebel."

"Smart girls get eaten all the time!" I complained, staring wide-eyed at the huge trees all around us, each rustle of leaves and every hoot of an owl making me even more nervous.

"Good girls *will* get eaten when they come out of the woods tomorrow morning," he replied with a simmering look.

I huffed, scowling at the dangerous woods. "That better be a promise, alpha."

Dean smirked, spanked my sore ass, and left me there in the whimpering woods to face whatever monsters the dark concealed.

10

I knew there were five other living, breathing people—well undead, breathing in the vampires' cases—in these woods with me, but the dark and the quiet were so complete as I trekked through the underbrush, I swore I was alone. A crow cawed somewhere in the distance, making me flinch, but the only other sounds I heard were my own trampling footsteps crushing branches under my boots.

Were the Discard Society still lurking about in these woods? I kinda wanted to join them and go on a murder spree. Just think of all the pretty pictures I could carve in those people.

But ... if I stayed in here, I wouldn't get the reward Dean promised me. *Or* get to see where this new bond with Slasher went.

No, I had to spend the night in the woods and leave in the morning. The upside was I wouldn't be sent to jail and shivved to death. I was a big fan of not being shivved to death.

"Bunny!" I gasped as a little brown rabbit crossed my path. A grin on my face, I crept after it, hoping there were ickle baby rabbits near its den. Would it let me pet them? I'd always wanted to pet a baby rabbit.

I skirted a huge wych elm tree and—where did the cute rabbit go? "Aw, that's not fair," I huffed, crossing my arms over my chest and shivering. It was getting cold, and the chill was cutting through my pink hoodie to rake its fingers across my chest. I should have worn a coat, or wheedled Dean out of his tweed jacket at least.

Thinking of Dean made my body heat, and I shivered harder, staring at the tangled trees around me. The darkness was so inky not even moonlight lit this part of the woods, but if I squinted, I could just make out the shapes of branches and leaves, and the roots stretching through the dirt beneath my boots.

A rough male cry echoed in the distance and I flinched, drawing two of my knives and pointing them at the darkness. Was that Vom becoming a midnight snack for nightmares? Dean had never said how many people came out of the woods versus how many died in here, but he wouldn't have left me if there was a chance I could die. Right?

I pricked my ears for more shouts, and swore my ears were more sensitive, that wolf senses were kicking in. But the only thing I heard was wind rustling the trees and the low hum of insects. I shivered, wishing Dean had come into the woods with me, wishing he'd stayed to protect me. But when have I ever needed someone else to keep me safe? I shook my head to clear it and did *not* think about insects as I pulled my hood up against the cold and gripped my knives tighter, moving deeper into the woods.

"Rebel," a quiet voice whispered near my ear, and I spun, slashing out at—

Nothing. There was nothing there.

My breath caught, and then came faster. There'd definitely been someone behind me, their voice so close to my ear. It sounded like ... like Ana. But Ana was dead; I'd been there, paralysed, listening to every horrific moment of her murder.

"Hide, Rebel," the voice said urgently, and I spun again, searching the darkness for her.

That *was* Ana. Was the woods full of ghosts? Is that what made people cry?

"Quickly, get under the bed, I'll deal with Kyle."

I started to shake, dim light bouncing off the edge of my knives as my hands trembled.

That was *Ana*, a voice I hadn't heard in five years, and I froze between one step and the next, the woods eerily quiet around me. Hairs rose all down my body and I strained my ears, waiting for the voice again.

"Don't argue, Rebel," she hissed. "Hide. I'll get rid of him."

I spun, pointing my shaking knife at the darkness. There was nothing there, but something was fucking with my senses.

"Come out, come out, little monster," I sang, ignoring the way my voice shook. "If you want to play, we can play."

But no beast crawled out of the underbrush, and no evil monkey jumped down from the trees. Which was a shame; monkeys were fluffy and cute, and I'd always wanted one as a sidekick. The monkey could distract my target while I slid up behind them and eased my knife across their throat.

I dragged a deep breath into my lungs and exhaled through my mouth. I'd faced these nightmares before; I could do it again now. If this was what I had to endure to avoid going to jail, I could do it.

"Quickly," Ana breathed again, her voice so close to my ear. I didn't spin this time, straining my ears for the sounds of cracking branches of footsteps rustling leaves and grass. There was nothing. I scanned the tree trunks next, half expecting a huge snake with whirly hypnotic eyes to be hugging one of them, playing tricks on my mind. "That's it, under the bed. I'll take him into the bathroom, and as soon as the door's shut, run to your room and lock the door, okay?"

I'd argued, had fought the whole time, knowing it was wrong, but Ana had been insistent and stubborn, and in the end the fear in her eyes had convinced me to crawl under the bed and hide while Kyle Ladislav stomped into the room and demanded to know why she was ignoring him. He'd been furious, worked into a rage by beer and hard spirits like usual, but it was worse since Ana had tried to break up with him the week before. He'd convinced her not to, and we'd still been stuck with him. I'd even tried to plead with Aunt Denise to *make* him leave us alone, but Kyle was a powerful witch from a powerful family. More important than Ana with her dregs of power and me with none.

I should have fought harder that day, should have figured out how to get my frozen limbs to crawl out from under the bed. Kyle had been my first kill, but I should have killed him *then*, not a year later when I'd finally worked up the nerve and the skills for it.

"Let's go in the shower," Ana said in the soft, calming voice she only used for him—because he was a bull likely to charge at any minute. He'd hit me before when I got in his way, even though I'd been thirteen. I knew that was why Ana told me to hide; she was trying to protect her little sister from a monster. But Kyle was more real a monster than anything that hid in my wardrobe.

The whimpering woods only echoed with my sister's voice, but I could hear Kyle's mean reply anyway, that whole day ingrained into my memory until I couldn't forget even a millisecond. "I don't want to fucking shower," he'd snarled, and Ana had cried out as he threw her onto the bed. "Word got out that you tried to end things with me," he'd said, the bed springs creaking above me as he climbed on. "The guys at the pub thought it was fucking hilarious. A pathetic witch like you trying to break things off with *me*."

"I'm sorry." Ana's voice echoed through the trees, lifting the hair from the back of my neck as if she was really here. My breath caught and I pointed my knife at the darkness, wishing I'd defended myself more vehemently when Dean said I'd be punished for Paulson's death. I should have thrown Slasher under the bus, even if he was my mate. A vampire would be better in this place of nightmares than me.

"You will be sorry," Kyle had growled. "Making a laughingstock of me. Me! Do you know how many women would kill to be in your place, Anabelle?"

I froze, waiting for her fatal words. I knew what her response was now, even if I hadn't understood then, had thought she was so *stupid* for arguing with him. This was the moment she snapped, fraying completely after months of abuse. I'd only seen the biggest, sharpest pieces of their relationship—the bruises, the shouts, the doors slamming, and his anger rebounding onto me. I hadn't seen the insidious subtleties, the daily manipulations, the constant destruction of her self-esteem, her mental health being shot to hell. Now, I could see the hints I'd been too young and sheltered to pick up then. Now, I could look back and see the trail that led to this moment. But I still wished I'd done something—anything—to prevent it. Instead of my bones locking as I hid under their bed, fear making me an icicle.

"My name is Anarchy."

Kyle had laughed; I could hear it in my skull even if the woods spared me the sound in my ears.

"My name," she repeated harder, "is *Anarchy*. It's what my mother called me; it's my name. Not Anabelle."

"Enough," I said to the woods, sheathing my knives so my hands were free as I marched for the nearest tree. "Enough, I get the fucking picture." I rocked back on my heels and then leapt, reaching up for the lowest branch, glad for the hours I'd spent working on my biceps in the gym as I hauled myself up. It still burned like hell, and I was out of breath by the time I flopped over the branch, but mission accomplished.

I allowed myself a single breath as Ana started to plead, trying futilely to calm her boyfriend down, and then I hauled myself up the next branch—and the next, and the next.

I didn't look down or my head would have gone all wobbly with dizziness. I kept my eyes fixed upward, on the next branch, until I'd climbed high enough to see the whole spread of the woods. And *still* I could hear Ana's voice, the ghost of her murder stalking me.

"Kyle," Ana rasped. "Can't—breathe."

He'd been ranting by then, going on and on about how his mates had laughed at him, had joked he couldn't even hold onto a dreg witch—a witch slur.

I shook my head hard, like I could dislodge the memory, the voices. "I get it, okay? That's enough now."

But it didn't stop. My eyes burned as I gripped the rough bark, my pink fingernails biting into the tree hard enough to embed dirt under them, my chest cinched tight with pain.

"Kyle, please..."

I'd fucking laid there, frozen, staring emptily. I hadn't even tried to get out from under the bed, hadn't tried to fight him. My body had locked down, and I *hated* myself for it. Even with Kyle dead and six feet under a human waste facility where he belonged, that hate never left me.

"Stop," Ana breathed, so faint it was barely audible. Her last word. It still rang in my ears most days, and it would for the rest of my life. Kyle had grunted in satisfaction that she'd finally shut up, and I'd screwed my eyes shut, the only movement my body would allow for long, long hours. I shuddered hard, breathing hard and fast at the memory. Rage built in my chest until I was itching to sink my knives into someone's body, needing to pour all my fury and grief out through violence, the cycle of death and blood endless.

I'd been young, but old enough to know what the sound of his belt buckle rattling meant, and tears had leaked out of my closed eyes. I'd screamed at my body, desperate to move, to save her, to hurt him. Instead, my body had betrayed me, and held me perfectly still while he raped my dead sister.

I didn't understand any of what I heard next, the rustling, the wet, gushy noises, and the huffs of exertion. It was only when I'd later crawl out from under the bed that I'd realise he'd cut her open.

And people wondered why I'd gone insane.

A bitter, broken laugh ripped from my lips now, and I pressed my head to the cold bark as it started to rain. I let the moisture drip down the back of my neck and soak through my hair, shaking at the memory rather than the chill.

I don't know how long I stayed up in that tree, my breathing broken and twisted laughs jerking my chest, completely out of my control. I needed to steal back control, needed to beat the shit out of the whimpering woods for torturing me. Or find the creature responsible for these hauntings and stab it in the dick. Or tits. Or general face area—anything gushy and painful.

The thought gave me a modicum of comfort, and I dragged myself back together long enough to descend the tree, carefully putting my feet on branches until I was on steady ground again. I ran before the nightmares could catch up to me again, but they followed, whispering in the voices of my Aunt Denise, and Antonella, and a dozen uncles, cousins, and aunts.

A waste of witch blood...

Useless dud...

Pathetic bitch...

Unworthy, unwanted, unloved...

I let it all slide through one ear and out the other, storming through the trees with my knives back in my hands, the act of crunching branches under my boots cathartic. Maybe I really would carve up a tree; I had a feeling it'd restore some inner calm. People ought to market that as a mental health retreat—spend time in nature, let the great outdoors soothe you, cut the guts out of a tree.

Each insult hit deep in the fragile flesh of my heart, but it didn't stop me trampling through the woods, furious enough to kill anyone who stepped across my path.

No killing the other Blake Hallies, I reminded myself. Dean would be pissy, and I'd probably be shipped off to prison. Not good.

Did you think we were going to live happily ever after?

I flinched hard at that one, my breath catching in my throat.

"You fucking arsehole," I hissed at the woods as I stomped past, pausing to kick a tree trunk and swearing viciously when my toes crumpled and stabbed with pain. "Goddamn trees, I'm going to burn down every single one of you the second I find a box of matches."

Why would I mate a dud?

"Because I'm brilliant and badass and, according to everyone I've slept with, actually quite pretty for a psycho," I shot back, wishing I could punch Edison's face. Now *that* would be extra cathartic. But I'd slashed him yesterday; I thought of that and smiled, ignoring the twinge in my chest. It went against my instincts to hurt my mate, but he'd hurt me first. Now we were almost even. Almost, because I still hadn't cut his dick off.

I don't want you. Why would I? I'm the most powerful heir to the Bray line.

"Most dickish heir to the Bray line," I muttered, but rubbed at the aching spot on my chest as I trudged on, my shoulders caving inward. It was too much—Edison's rejection, my family's loathing, and Ana's death. It was too much, and I was going to snap.

My breathing ruptured and split into painful shards, each one cutting up my lungs, my heart, but I kept walking because moving was better than standing still. I'd frozen once; I couldn't do it again. Wouldn't let myself stop.

I was a self-trained kickass killer—

And a grade A fucking idiot! I gasped at the *click* beneath my boot and screamed as air whooshed down from above. A crude cage of sharpened planks of wood swung down too fast for me to avoid, the tips of every single one sharp enough to rip my body apart. I should know; I was an expert on carving up bodies. My breath caught in my chest as I lurched away from the spikes, too slow, too fucking slow—

A solid weight slammed into my side and knocked me aside so fast that the world blurred and my scream roared. I flew, or that was how it felt, and the cage thudded into the ground, the sharp stakes sinking deep into the dirt. I could have been pulp and broken bones. *Would* have been if I hadn't flown.

How...?

I swayed, my stomach twisting unpleasantly until I bent at the waist and vomited on the grass, bile burning my throat. "Ugh," I rasped, wiping my mouth on my hoodie sleeve and watching the trees swirl and dance around me.

"It's okay, you're okay, tiramisu, you're okay."

I laughed, relief hitting me so hard I wobbled.[1] "Slasher," I breathed, letting him pull me against his body as dizziness raged through me. "You saved me."

He held me tighter, a vicious hiss leaving his throat as he nuzzled the top of my head. "You almost died, my beautiful Pringle."

I sagged against his wiry-strong body, a smile on my face as the world stopped spinning around me. I'd always wondered what travelling at vampire speed felt like, and now I knew: like fairground teacups, a crazy rollercoaster, and a tumble dryer all rolled into one nauseating experience. I felt alarmingly like a hamster thrown into one of those candy-coloured exercise balls.

"What the hell are the advisors playing at?" I growled, winding my arms around Slasher's waist and snuggling, letting his bristling violence soothe me. "Putting murder cages like that in the woods?"

"Good question," my vampire mate hissed, hugging me even tighter. "I'm going to find whoever put that trap there and rip them into a million bloody pieces."

I swooned. "I'll help you."

I swore Slasher swooned too; he let out a dreamy sigh that fanned the small hairs near my scalp. "Are you all right, bubblegum?" He pulled back, scanning me with intense red eyes. I could barely see him in the darkness, but there was enough moonlight to see the vicious worry cutting his sculpted face, making his mania even more manic.

I rolled onto my tiptoes and pressed a kiss to his lips, smiling when he kissed me back so fiercely his fangs nipped my bottom lip. His tongue swept over the stinging hurt and he groaned deeply, his hands dropping to my ass and squeezing.

"Don't think you're getting more than kisses," I warned him, gasping between vicious presses of his lips to mine. "There are *things* in these woods."

"I'll kill every single creature that hunts you," he swore, his fangs bared and his eyes glowing a deep red. He looked so deadly and vampiric that I grinned and cupped his face, tracing his devastating bone structure—his deep brows, his cutting cheeks, his straight nose, his firm jaw.

"I know you will," I replied, darting forward to run my tongue along the sharp edge of his fang. He groaned, slamming his hips into mine and grinding tight. "But I meant it's full of *insects*." I didn't have to fake my shudder.

"I'll kill all those, too," he promised, trembling under my touch. "I'm so hungry, Jelly Baby."

Butterflies burst to life in my belly. "I like that name."

"I like you," he replied, ducking his head to lick my throat. "And how you smell. I bet I'd like how you taste, too."

"Bite me," I breathed, sliding my fingers into his long, black hair. "But don't take much; I need to be strong enough to last in these woods until morning."

"I'll protect you," he purred, his voice low and hypnotic now, his tongue flat to my pulse. "And so will your stalker."

I reared back, my eyes flying wide and alarm bright in my chest. "What do you mean, my stalker?"

"I'm not the only man watching you in these woods," Slasher murmured, sliding his body back along mine and sucking a particularly amazing spot on my neck. My fingers clutched his hair hard and I groaned. "There's a wolf, too. Big and strong and broody."

Was ... was Dean watching over me? My eyes stung.

"Please can I bite you now, my delicious Nutella?"

I laughed at this name, but that was flattering as hell. Nutella was the best and tastiest food mankind had ever invented. "You can bite me, vampy."

He didn't hesitate, and I gasped as sharp fangs sank into my throat, twin throbs of pain punching through me before turning to a low, simmering burn. The sinful moan Slasher let out against my neck was so hot that I endured the burn, gripping his dark hair tight as he took long, hard pulls of my blood.

I'd just started to go floaty and dazed when a loud scream echoed in the distance, and Slasher's head snapped up with a deadly hiss. He held me tight to his body, his upper lips curled back from his fangs, the sharp points dripping my blood. He looked ready to make good on his promise to kill everything in these woods.

"That's ... twice I've heard someone ... scream," I slurred, nuzzling my face against his shoulder and taking his sharp, spicy scent into my lungs.

"You're not staying in these woods," Slasher snarled. "Someone's hunting you all."

I batted his back in a weak slap. "If I leave before sunrise, I'll get kicked out of Blake Hall."

Slasher's hiss was louder this time, and so fierce that a shiver tripped down my spine. My pussy dripped, a completely inappropriate reaction. But when had I ever cared about silly things like being appropriate? "Fuck," he spat, his hand splaying across my back.

The same scream from before ripped the air, and I startled, the shock clearing some of the pleasant daze from Slasher's bite when the sound cut off abruptly. Silence rang around us. I stared into the darkness, wishing I had vampire vision but glad I had my own personal guide vampire with me.

"I'll be fine," I breathed. "I've got six knives, and my scary, crazy vampire to keep me safe."

"Aww," he breathed, his eyes so big and full of love as he gazed down at me, his sharp-nailed fingers cupping my cheek. "You think I'm scary?"

"The scariest," I promised, leaning onto my tiptoes for more kisses. Yeah, people were screaming around us and probably getting killed by deadly cages—or worse—but it was still the perfect moment for a hard make-out session.

I gasped as air whipped past me and my back slammed into a tree trunk, Slasher's cool lips demanding on mine. His tongue forced mine into submission in the most delicious way. My toes curled in my boots and I rubbed against him like a kitty, sending a shivery sensation through my nipples.

"*My* french fry," he snarled against my lips, diving back in for another forceful kiss that made my stomach flutter with delighted butterfly wings. "Mine." He sucked my bottom lip, teasing me with the sharp point of his fang. "Mine." His lips caught my tongue and suctioned hard, sending a shudder down my spine and my hands clutching him more insistently. "All mineminemine."

I grinned, my heart melty and soft at his obsessive claiming. It felt damn good to be wanted after hearing my family's —and Edison's—constant, ruthless rejection. So I dug my fingernails into the back of Slasher's neck and kissed him back every bit as hard.

He'd saved me from the trap that would have crushed my body and savagely ended my life, and I didn't let myself think about the men's screams and shouts of terror, didn't let myself think about how close I'd come to meeting the same gruesome end.

11

I staggered out of the thick tree cover of the whimpering woods the second the sky began to lighten, my head in a daze and the terror of the male screams rattling around my skull. Slasher had given me a deep, underwear-melting kiss at the first rays of dawn, and left as soon as he saw me to safety. Like the other vampires, he had a witch's potion charm that allowed him to be out in the sun, but it still drained his energy and felt like being stung by a thousand bees all at once. Not a fun situation for my psychotic darling vampire.

"Dean!" I breathed when I spotted him pacing the edge of the woods, his silver hair sticking up in places like he'd run his hands through it and his tweed suit horribly rumpled. He looked good like this, unkempt and tempting. My pussy throbbed a message in morse code I was pretty sure spelled out g-i-v-e. m-e. c-o-c-k. "You waited for me," I said, and threw myself at him with my arms outstretched.

His shoulders sagged a second before he caught me, holding me so tight he threatened to bruise. I wiggled against him, all turned on and needy from a night of making out with Slasher, and locked my hands behind his neck. He shocked me by running his hand over my tangled pink curls and holding me close in silence, his chest expanding with a deep breath like he was sucking down my scent. Usually I smelled of vanilla and honey,[1] but I knew I must stink of dirt and leaves now. Dean didn't seem to mind, he breathed me in and shuddered.

"What's wrong?" I asked, a deep V between my brows as I put a tiny bit of space between us, scanning his lined, scruffy face for clues.

"What's *wrong?*" he demanded in a growl, his whiskey eyes flashing. "We heard screams all fucking night, Rebel. I thought it was you."

I huffed, giving him a sulky look. "I said I wouldn't hurt anyone; it was one of your rules, remember?"

"Baby, I thought the screams were *yours*," he rumbled, all guttural and deep and shiver-inducing.

"Oh," I breathed, sliding my hands up his arms to his impressive biceps. "You were worried about me," I realised, and knew my eyes must have been like Slasher's when he gave me his heart-eyed stare. "I knew you liked me, Sexy Sir."

He didn't respond to my teasing. "You're my mate," he snarled, his lip curled back from his sharp canines and his chest jerking with fast breaths. "You might be a brat and a pain in the ass, but you're my mate, and I'm supposed to keep you *safe*."

"I am safe," I pointed out cheerfully, my fingers continuing their quest of mapping his body as they dove down the strong slope of his back.

"No thanks to me," he growled. "I sent you in there, to face fuck knows what was causing those screams."

"But you followed me," I replied, blinking up at him. "Right?"

Confusion tightened his features, and surprise lit up my insides like fireworks on Bonfire Night. "No, baby," he replied, something like guilt in his eyes, turning down the corners of his mouth. I'd have to fix that with a long, heated kiss, but first...

"If you weren't the wolf following me through the woods," I mused, a cool shiver skating down my back, "then who was stalking me?"

12

I'd come across the other residents of Blake Hall while getting food from the dining room, and walking the hallways, but I'd never seen them all in one place like this. A quick count told me there were thirty-seven of us gathered in the wide, dimly lit foyer—the only space big enough to hold everyone. Confused murmurs echoed off the high ceiling, muffled by the tapestries on the walls, and impatient steps squeaked on the tiled floor.

I bit my lip, feeling out of place as I followed the last few people into the foyer, immediately aware that everyone stood in one of three groups: the wolves all banded together in the Crescent Club, the witches stood in a Mystic Club huddle, and the vampires of the Crimson Club lounged separately but all vaguely together by the huge paintings on the far wall.

Hang on a minute...

I squinted at the middle painting of a black-haired man with a pale, aquiline face and a proud, haughty smirk. He was dressed in a see-through white shirt and a jazzy red cravat, and I was almost a hundred percent sure[1] it was my Slasher.

I would have gone to stand beside it to inspect the portrait if that wasn't clearly the designated Crimson Club spot. Did having a vamp mate qualify me to hang out with them? I didn't know. Didn't think so.

Ughhhh, I hated this. It was like being back at Falcon Manor all over again. I'd walked away from this bullshit. I didn't want a clique or a club; I wanted to go back to my life of gorging on doughnuts during the day and stalking victims at night.

I ended up picking a spot next to a marble bust of Gloriella Blake, the apparent co-founder of this dumb hall, and crossed my arms over my chest, giving a warning scowl to anyone who dared to stare at me. I felt like a circus exhibit. *Roll up, roll up, see the one-of-a-kind dual-blood. Under the full moon, she grows a fuzzy tail and super cute ears. In theory, she can cast spells like any other witch—behold the marvel!* One more stare and I was going to do a handstand and wiggle my toes at them in a wave.

And anyway, I wasn't the only dual-blood in the world, or there wouldn't be a name for it. I was rare, and the stuck-up witches didn't like to think about interspecies couples, but they were real, and so were their kids.

Why hadn't my mum told me who my real dad was? Had Ana known? The thought of her keeping a secret stabbed deep into my heart, but I focused on my breathing and moved past it. Everything Ana had done was to protect me; if she'd kept a secret, it was because the truth would have put me in danger.

If everyone had known I was a witchy wolf back then, would I have been sent to Blake Hall as a kid? I'd never have survived the whimpering wood as a ten-year-old. No way in hell.

But the only reason I was here *now* was because some dumbass seer said I had volatile, dangerous magic that risked the lives of nice, innocent paranormals. So where the hell *was* my magic?

"Quiet, now," a melodious, feminine voice called above the chatter, and the conversations halted mid-word as the jailors—tutors—advisors[2] walked down the dark staircase, halting on the carpeted steps above us. Nice—reminding us of our place in society. I scanned the advisors until I found Dean and smirked when I saw him already watching me, his gaze intent. I hadn't expected there to be many plus points of spending a night in a nightmare-infested wood, but I liked this ultra protectiveness from my alpha mate. I liked it a lot. My imagination provided me with the image of him stalking down those carpeted steps, grabbing me, and throwing me up against the wall. Pulling down my jeans and fucking me there while everyone stared in horror or surprise or arousal. Showing everyone I was his and he was mine, all mine.

I shook my head to clear the fantasy, and realised the woman at the top of the steps was talking.

"—to tell you that three residents lost their lives during a routine trial."

A routine trial! Reliving my sister's murder was *routine?* I gnashed my teeth, planning murder as I narrowed my gaze on the striking dark-skinned woman. She must have been the head jailor of this place, the rehabilitation warden or chief babysitter—whatever the hell she went by. Electric blue braids flowed to her lower back, her eyeshadow and lipstick in a matching shade, and she wore a black corseted dress that wouldn't have been out of place at Whitby's goth weekend. She was cool in a dangerous kinda way, but I would still get stabby with her if she kept belittling my nightmarish trial.

I was too busy being angry to hear much of what my 'neighbours' said in response, their murmurings background noise to the memories of my sister's murder.

"I'll ask you to stay out of the woods while we investigate what happened, and try not to panic. We'll find the culprit and deal with them swiftly and without mercy."

A chill of excitement went down my spine. Dean said he was in charge of punishment; would my alpha get all murdery when he found whoever set those traps?

"If any of you know anything, come to my office in the tower any time before dawn." I blinked. Before dawn? Was she a vampire? "And I want everyone who was in the woods last night to provide a statement."

"You don't think one of them killed those people?" one of the witches asked, strangely non-snooty thanks to the fear in her voice. "Are we safe in here with them?"

"I vote we kick them out, let them stay in the woods if they're going to go around killing everyone."

I rolled my eyes. But my curiosity did blink open its eyes. Who had made it out? Were the wolves dead, or had one of the vampires died? I bet Boyband was still alive; he seemed like the annoying type who never knew when to die.

"Don't be ridiculous," the blue-haired woman in charge cut in, heavy on condescension. "Any more talk like that and *you'll* be the ones moving into the woods."

That shut the witches up. I smirked, crossing my arms over my chest, but I felt eyes prickling the side of my face. I glared across the foyer at the Mystic Club, and my blood went cold when I saw *who* was burning holes in my skull with his evil black eyes. I let all my revenge-y thoughts show through my eyes as I glared across the lobby at Edison. He quickly looked away, his mouth pressed thin, and victory burned like a fire in my chest.

"Is it the Discard Society?" a deep-voiced wolf asked, somewhere from the huddle of wolves. I supposed they were a pack all their own, bonded by rejection and crime. Or future-crime. It was unfair that we were all here because some seer saw we'd be dangerous. What if the seer was a fraud? I was definitely a danger to society, but I wasn't going to murder with my *magic*.[3]

"Don't be absurd," huffed the chief advisor lady I really ought to learn the name of. "The Discard Society was an inflated rumour in the eighties. They were two people who messed around with blood magic, and they were both killed years ago."

I gasped, my mouth popping open.

Blood magic?

I made a squeak of excitement that drew some weird stares, but I didn't care. I neeeeeeded to learn blood magic. Could I make my *My Little Pony* carvings come to life and dance around a corpse's chest?

Yet more reasons to find this Discard Society and join them. Although if they were back, and were trying to kill us, I'd have to kill them first. They'd nearly gored me in a wooden cage; they definitely needed to die a horrible, bloody death.

Interesting how quickly Blue-Haired Lady had shot down the wolf's theory, too. Was there some truth to the rumours?

"Trialists from last night, follow me to my office."

Ooh, trialists. That was a fun name.

And yep, out of the throng of vampires strolled Boyband, full of confidence and smugness. I hid a tiny fist pump.

Called it! Dauntley was notably absent, though. *Damn*, the killer had taken down a vampire. I was impressed.

I squeezed through a huddle of wolves, moving in the direction of the steps, fully intending to brush past Dean on my way up the steps and accidentally rub my ass on his crotch. But before I could reach the staircase, a massive hand closed around my upper arm and yanked me into a dark corridor, flattening my back to an unfamiliar—and huuuuge—chest.

"Um," I said, subtly feeling for one of my knives. "Hi?"

"Tell Ivelle the person who set traps is woman. Taller than you, Little Scorpion. Long hair, pale colour."

"What?" I asked dumbly, fighting his unmovable hold on me. Damn, he was big. I tilted my head back and gawped at the vague shadow of a head two feet above mine. Woaahhhh, he was a giant. And annoyingly concealed by the dimness. I wanted to see his face. Was this my mysterious stalker? "Who are you?"

I slashed down with my knife, aiming for his thigh,[4] but his hands tightened on my arms and he spun me back into the foyer. When I pointed my knife back down the corridor, it was empty.

"Dammit," I hissed, goosebumps covering my arms where his fingers had pressed into muscle and skin.

The killer was a woman? But who the hell was she, and why was she trying to kill the residents of Blake Hall?

13

a day later, I was climbing the walls. If this place had been anything like a prison or an academy, I might have had something to *do*—lessons to not pay attention to and laundry to ignore while gossiping or making out with my Slasher. But instead we were left to our own devices, trapped within the iron gates of Blake Hall's grounds and watched by the advisors constantly. Wherever I went, eyes burned into my back; it had taken me this long to realise it wasn't the other residents, or even my stalker watching me, but the watchmen who prowled the corridors. Who all answered to Dean and Ivelle—Blue-Haired Lady.

I wondered if Dean had told them to keep a closer eye on me; he'd been ultra protective when I emerged from the whimpering woods. Not that he'd bothered to come find me all yesterday *or* today. I'd been left by myself, and it was starting to make me crazy.[1]

I'd even gone into the television room and hung out in the window seat I'd promptly thrown a witch out of, claiming the spot for myself. But apparently the Mystic Club got pissy when you gave a witch a concussion and then threatened to stab their leader's eyes out with your sharp, pink fingernails. Sensitive people, witches. Good thing Edison hadn't been there, or I'd have cut his balls off if he'd even looked at me.

I flopped onto my bed, my skin crawling with inactivity. I needed to *do* something.

"I'm *bored*," I whined out loud.

The next trial had been postponed for a few days, and I didn't have another how-to-use-magic session with Vivian until tomorrow. Slasher was napping while the sun was up, and I'd yet to make any besties in either Crescent or Mystic Club—although I wasn't holding out much hope, since neither seemed to want anything to do with a dual-blood—so I was left talking to myself.

"You know what would make you feel better?" I asked myself.

"I don't know, Other Rebel," I replied, staring up at my cream ceiling, the lightbulb humming loudly. "What *would* make me feel better?"

"Finding someone to hunt," I replied, my heart already picking up at the thought.

"But I don't have any jobs out here, and none of my contacts know where to find me thanks to stupid Dean basically kidnapping me," I huffed.

"You don't need a job to kill someone," Other Rebel pointed out. Intelligent woman, that Other Rebel. I liked her.

"Good point," I agreed, sitting up in a rush as a grin crossed my face. "I bet we could find someone mean and dickish to murder. We'd be doing a public service, really, ridding the world of someone gross."

Other Rebel didn't reply, but that was fine, because my mind was already racing with opportunities. Everything was dull today, and I was still shaky from the list of crazy shit that had happened to me, for example:

1. Being sent into a scary woods to fend for myself against monsters that maaaaybe wanted to eat me.
2. Being forced to relive every traumatic nightmare that had driven me gradually crazy until one day my mind snapped and the old, sane Rebel went bye-bye.
3. Nearly getting impaled to death by a big, stakey cage.
4. Being stalked by a huuuuge, scary wolf who believed it was a woman who'd set the traps and killed two wolves and a vamp.[2]

Bruises had formed in a billion places across my body, and not all of them were fun ones left by my possessive mates. My stalker had left a ring of fingerprints around my upper arm like a tattoo, and my almost-death left a bunch of hurty places from Slasher slamming into me.

Not to mention my heart felt a little bruised, and my grief over losing Ana had wrapped around my throat like a permanent noose. I needed to feel more like myself again, and sinking into bloodlust always made me feel better. Other Rebel was right; I needed to kill something. Well, some*one*. Animals were too cute to hurt. People were horrible.

Really, everyone ought to thank me for getting rid of the worst ones.

I stripped out of my pale pink vest and blue jeans, flicking through the hangers in my new wardrobe. I hadn't had time to pack many things, but at least I'd brought the essentials. I pulled on my black skinny jeans, my dark hoodie, and zipped it up over an equally inky shirt. I'd been living my best pastel bubblegum fantasy lately with all my clothes cerise, rose, and flamingo, but I was still head over heels in love with black, the perfect echo of my corrupted soul. It felt good to be decked head to toe in ominous jet, like my clothes were a warning to everyone to back the fuck off.

I grinned as I hid my favourite knives in my waistband, my boot, and strapped one to my back beneath my hoodie. I swore I could breathe easier when I set off out of my room, stalking down the corridor with my murder bag slung over my shoulder.

Most of the witches took one look at me and kept out of my way, but the wolves rumbled growls as I passed, like they could sense the threat in me. I batted my eyelashes at them and swung my hips as I sauntered past. The vampires mostly ignored me, which was kinda rude, but I already had one vampire mate so I stuck my tongue out at them and kept walking.

"Where are you going?" a tinkling voice demanded. Oh good, Daisy, the head witch was back for round two. I strode past her down the gloomy hallway, aiming for a door I'd found that exited near the back of the hall.

"Bulgaria," I replied arily, and snorted at her pinched expression. Why were witches always so sneery? Didn't they know their faces would stick that way? "Or maybe Japan. I haven't decided yet."

"You can't just *leave*," she blurted. "It's against the rules."

I rolled my eyes and ignored my whiny shadow's complaints. "Who died and made you prison warden?"

"I'm the most powerful Mystic Club member—"

"Good for you, love." I reached the door and pulled it

open, blessed nighttime air biting my exposed skin, filling my lungs in a rush of comfort and familiarity.

"Which means everything you do reflects on my witches and me, and I won't—"

I slammed the door on her face with a snort, and skipped down the slope towards the road and the gates.

14

The dumbasses who ran Blake Hall hadn't even enchanted the gates or the iron fence that surrounded the property. I snickered at their stupidity as I scaled the fence, dropped down on the other side, and skipped in the direction of the nearest village. Villages had pubs, and pubs had people being assholes; that was basic maths. I just needed to find the meanest asshole and sink my knife into their jugular. All my shakiness and jittery boredom would float away at the first spray of blood, I knew it.

The cool breeze lifted pink curls from my forehead, and I lifted my face into the cold as I slowed, enjoying the feeling of fresh air on my face after a whole day cooped up in my room. It felt good to be on the hunt again, to be stalking my prey as the sun slid below the horizon, even if I didn't know *who* my prey was like normal. It was weird not to have a client waiting for confirmation, and weirder still to know I wasn't going to get paid for the kill. But recalibrating my mood would be all the payment I needed. This was basically a mental health retreat.[1]

I couldn't believe how easy it had been to break out of Blake Hall, but I wasn't complaining. Still, it was the home to criminals and bad guys who needed training and trials to become nice, normal human beings.[2] You'd *thiiink* they might want to put some security around the parameter. A nice, big floodlight that would flash on and blind anyone trying to climb the fence. A blaring siren that made ears bleed. A super mysterious elite team of guards who'd drag the escapee back to Blake Hall.

I was a little insulted, honestly. And more than disappointed. I wanted a challenge, something to make my blood roar and my heart pound.[3] If Blake Hall had been an actual prison, I might have had something to occupy my mind, but there was no ignoring the downside of incarceration: shivving, sleeplessness, and gang politics. Even juvie had been more exciting than Blake Hall, and that was taking into account the murder cages in the woods. No chores, no be-a-better-person training, and not even a murder-inducing psychiatrist session. At least *then* I'd have had someone to talk to, someone to unleash my anger and fear upon.

Wait, *fear?*

I paused at the top of a hill overlooking a small cluster of lights cupped in a grassy valley, searching through the buzzing noise in my head, feeling around the pinching in my chest. Was I afraid? Was that why I'd been restless and agitated all day?

Huh. Maybe Blake Hall was working after all. I was having a normal person reaction. Go me!

I dragged in a deep breath, tasting the sharp tang of night air and green, growing things—probably the trees lining the path, but I wasn't about to go lick one to find out. I was *scared*, and I didn't like the feeling. I was used to being a total in-control badass, not an out-of-her-depth badass. But there was a murderer loose in Blake Hall's grounds, and while that wouldn't normally bother me, I'd almost been killed. It had almost been *my* life slashed short, *my* blood spilling, *my* bones shattered.

I needed to rally my courage and hunt down the killer before I could get caught up in their murder plot again, but the fear stood in my way, looming over me like ... like my stalker. Could he be the killer? He'd said it was a blonde woman, but that could be complete bullshit.

I shivered, forcing myself to resume walking even as my mind dove back into memories of Kyle, of the sharp, biting chill that had spread through me whenever he was in one of his moods, when his eyes would land on me and narrow, and I'd know I was in danger. I wouldn't go back to that; I refused to be little and scared again.

I couldn't be the same girl who'd cowered under the bed while her sister was murdered and brutalised.

I refused to be.

And the first step to being better, braver, and deadlier was to remind myself who I really was. Not Rebecca Falcon, but Rebel Falcon—Graves. I'd never really been Rebecca anyway; my mum always called me Rebel, and always called Ana Anarchy. Rebecca and Anabelle were ghosts, and I was glad to leave them haunting Falcon Manor while I moved on.

But that was the damn trouble: no matter how far forward I moved, those ghosts always dogged my steps, calling out in their chilling voices.

I drew a serrated knife from my spine as I reached the village, pulling my sleeve over my hand to hide it as I wove around thatched cottages and quaint rows of terraces, each with blooming window boxes and lacquered doors.

Ah.

Finding a target might be a teensy bit harder than I expected, since this place was postcard-perfect. Harder, but not impossible. I knew well enough the monsters who hid among wealth and prettiness were as bad as those who lurked in squalor and poverty. Worse, for the masks they wore and the smiles that convinced people they were trustworthy.

I kept my shoulders back as I strolled past the houses, conveying confidence even if I twisted with doubt inside, trying to wrangle my self esteem back. Up ahead, a cluster of weathered stone buildings leaned together. The little shop and post office were dark, closed up for the night, but light blazed like a beacon from the warped windows of the Golden Fleece.

I grinned. Perfect.

Buzzing with excitement, I tucked my hood tighter around my face and scanned the street, searching for a place to hide. I settled on a shadowy snicket opposite the pub, between a village hall and a dark butcher shop. My heart beating fast, I tucked myself into the mouth of the path and eyed the pub across the way. I knew exactly what I was looking for, had seen the same mean, thuggish look in enough eyes over the years to spot them in strangers I'd never laid eyes on before. Someone, somewhere would thank me—a battered child or abused spouse or fearful employee. If someone had come along and killed Kyle when I was a kid, I would have thanked them, and Ana would still be alive.

Purpose straightened my spine and kicked my doubt in the face, and I settled into the excitement of the hunt. This was the hardest bit—waiting for my target to come into view—but I'd done it long enough to know the fun parts were worth the dull wait.

Minutes later, the pub door opened across the street with a rusty creak and my mood perked up, my focus honed like a razor's edge. The road was narrow enough for me to make out the faces of the two men who emerged from the inn, the collars of their coats pulled up against worn, lined faces and deep set eyes. One of them was small and hunched, in a black wax jacket, the other taller and proud. The angle of his chin made my interest peak, something haughty and cocky about it, and my blood pounded faster at the potential target.

I shook out my hands so my body was nice and tensionless, tracing my thumb lovingly over the handle of my knife, ready to stalk my maybe-target.

But a *whoosh* of air behind me had me tensing on instinct, and I spun at the quiet thud of a landing. Whoever had snuck up on me knew how to land quietly; if I hadn't been on high alert, I might have missed the low scrape of boots on stone.

I was already moving, my knife angled low for a deep, gutting blow—but I halted as the figure came into focus in the faint light from the navy blue sky. Tall and broad shouldered in a black coat and trousers, with a stubbled square jaw and heavy brows drawn low.

"Uh oh," I breathed as Dean rose out of his crouch, moving deadly fast with those beautiful whiskey-brown eyes fixed on me, glowing with a predatory gleam.

"You thought you could run away, Miss Falcon?" His laugh was low and full of scorn as he stalked the few steps towards me, only pausing when I lifted my beautiful, serrated knife[4] and pointed it at him. The knife was custom made, and special to me, and I loved her. "Silly girl."

"Do I *look* like I'm running away?" I hissed, rolling my eyes hard.

He paused to scan me, from my hood, to my black clothes, to the knife I was aiming at him, and his mouth twisted with confusion.

"And I *am* a silly girl," I went on, aware that every second I spoke my maybe-target was getting away. Dammit. "I'm proud of being silly, and even prouder of being a girl. So if you wanted to insult me, bad luck, Sexy Sir."

He went still, and that stillness made my hackles rise, the wolfie part of me recognising the danger of his alertness. "If you're not running away, what are you doing here?"

"Stress relieving," I replied with an annoyed shrug. "Now can you leave me alone? I was a teensy bit busy before you distracted me with this growly guard act." I gestured with the knife. "Go on, go away."

His head reared back, insult and offense flaring his brown eyes, and a twinge of regret tightened my chest. "Why do you have a knife, Rebel?" he asked, harsh and no-nonsense.

"Uhh, for fun. Duh!" I shook my head in exasperation, twisting to peek down the road at the two men. Annnd, they were gone. Perfect. I huffed a growl, facing Dean again with a dark scowl. "Which you just *ruined*, you big, sexy killjoy. Thanks for that."

"Who are you watching?" he demanded, and muscled past me, his big hand burning my hip as he pushed me aside and looked down the street. I tapped his shoulder with the sharp tip of my lovely Tina, a silent warning that I was getting sliiightly irritated. "What the hell are you doing here, Rebel?"

"I prefer it when you call me baby or Miss Falcon," I purred, trailing the knife down his jacket, light enough to not cut him. "We should play teacher and student some time. But not now; now I've got things to do and you're getting in the way. So vamoose."

He raised a thick brow, the tiniest corner of his mouth daring to curl. "Vamoose?"

"It means get out of my way, you big lug," I huffed, tapping him a little harder with Tina's sharp edge. His gaze snagged on my knife and stuck there, and I resisted the urge to stab him[5] as he snapped his hand up and gripped my wrist, pulling the knife away from his shoulder so he could scrutinise it.

"Where did you get this, Miss Falcon?"

"See," I breathed, shivering at his low, growly voice. "Much hotter when you call me that."

"Answer the question," he snapped, baring his sharp canines. But his grip on my wrist never became painful, and his wicked teeth didn't scare me.

"I bought it," I replied petulantly. "Satisfied?"

Dean let go of me abruptly, and my hand fell. I managed to avoid stabbing myself in the thigh only thanks to my quick reflexes—and only got my hand up fast enough to stop the bigger, thicker dagger aimed at my chest because of all my training.

"You're fast and observant," he noted, although I had a feeling he was mostly talking to himself. We danced down the dark, dead-end path, me deflecting his fast strikes. My heart started to race, thumping against my ribs, and my blood sang. Finally! This was what I'd been missing all day, what I'd been dying to have while I was bored out of my skull.

"You're cold, you eat people, and you sparkle in the sun," I joked with a bright laugh, not caring to keep my voice down anymore. I didn't care if I gave my position away; I'd find another target tomorrow. For now, this was getting interesting.

"Hilarious," Dean replied flatly, bringing his dagger around in an arc that had my breath catching, bright light leaping off my knife as it scraped along his own weapon.

"Woahhhhh," I gasped, stepping back and disengaging for a second. "Did you see that? Tell me you saw that!"

"I saw it," he replied, giving me a strange look I couldn't interpret. Not annoyed or aroused. More ... baffled. "You knew you had magic, Rebel."

"I know," I breathed, my excitement growing. "But I've never seen it before! That was *awesome!*"

Dean laughed a soft sound, and his eyes focused, losing that confused sheen. I loved the way he smiled at me, one side of his mouth kicked up higher than the other, lines cutting deep around his eyes.

"February 26th 2019," he said, still smiling.

"Huh?" I tilted my head, not sure why that date was important.

"A farmer found a thirty-something woman dead and mutilated in his field. Her red hair was like fire against the crops and her blood and guts even redder."

I blinked, my eyes wide and my heart kicking up. That hadn't been mine. Right...? I was pretty sure it wasn't. I'd have remembered that.

"July 1st 2020," he went on, his eyes bright. "A pale, auburn woman was strung up to a scarecrow's post, her throat slit so blood spilled down her naked body and her stomach slashed, entrails hanging artfully from the gaping wound."

My breath caught. "I remember that one! All the papers started calling the killer the Straw Man, which is the coolest name I've ever heard. I'm kinda jealous, actually."

His smile softened to something like affection that made my stomach squirmy and my heart melt. I lowered my knife, taking a step closer to him. He spun his long dagger and sheathed it along his back in a dizzying move that made me swoon into him. My breaths came short and sharp as his arms wrapped around me, exhilaration burning through me. I started to put Tina away, but he halted me with a caress down my wrist. "Keep it out."

I raised an eyebrow.

He just continued, "January 5th 2021. Another meadow, another scarecrow post. This woman was older, and looked so similar to my mother. She was killed and gutted in the same way as the second, her intestines arranged perfectly, her eyes open and unseeing as the birds came to pick at her."

I trailed a hand up his muscular chest, rolling onto my tiptoes to whisper against his ear, "What are you saying, Dean?"

"I'm saying," he replied, his hot hand splayed against my spine, "I recognise that knife, Graves."

A bright burst of laughter left my lips and I dropped back to my feet, sharing up at him with wide eyes. "Woah, wait! *You're* the Straw Man!"

He inclined his head, a smug smile playing about his mouth. "Everyone Graves has killed in the past three years has been cut in some way by a very specific, unique knife. One, the sketches say, looks just like that knife there."

"Tina," I informed him, holding her up proudly. "She's a custom made beauty. A birthday present for myself." I beamed up at him, something like happiness bubbling up inside me. "Are you really...?"

"I really am," he agreed, his hands moving up and down my back, a scorching contrast to the chill. "Are you Graves, the contract killer who's slaughtered more people in the past year than anyone else in the country?"

I swooned. Genuinely tipped forward into him, my heart going pitter-patter. "You've heard of me."

"*You've* heard of *me*," he replied with a sharper grin. He ducked his head and laid a kiss to the bite mark that had left a white scar on my shoulder. "You're completely unhinged. I suspected that before, but knowing you're Graves..."

"Says the man who makes living scarecrows," I replied snarkily, like that wasn't the coolest fucking thing *ever*. And the way he'd talked about those murders, the explicit details and the excitement in his voice... I was swooning again, lightheaded as my blood raced.

"You carved children's cartoons into people's bodies," he countered. "While they were alive."

"You say that like it's in the past," I laughed, tilting my head back to look at him, my handsome wolf, my sexy mate, my—my serial killer. My stomach erupted with butterflies and didn't stop fluttering for *ever*. "The only thing that stopped me making more pretty pictures was you interrupting my hunt tonight."

His whiskey eyes flared like pure gold, a canine tooth poking free as he grinned. "You're just perfect, aren't you, baby?"

I swallowed, my eyes wide at the reverence shining from his. "Just as perfect as you, my Straw Man."

He cupped my cheek in a big hand, his thumb caressing my cheekbone. "I'll find you another kill, baby. A better one than that boring husband."

My eyes stung, tears building. "That's the sweetest thing anyone's ever said to me."

He held my body close to his and lowered his head for a passionate, heartbreakingly gentle kiss. "I'll find you someone who'll put up a bigger fight. From all the post mortem reports of your victims, you only carve up the ones with defensive wounds on their hands and wrists."

A body-wide shudder shook me and I pressed fully against him, goosebumps covering me all over.

He laughed softly, running his thumb over my bottom lip. "You gonna come, baby? You look like you're in heaven."

I sucked his thumb into my mouth, moaning at the salty tang of his skin. "So much heaven," I groaned around his thumb. "More heavenly than heaven."

Dean laughed and pressed a sweet kiss to my forehead. "How about I give you something even better to suck on, my beautiful assassin?"

"Gimme, gimme," I gasped, letting go of his thumb with a last, wet suck and dropping to my knees on the dirty stone path. I didn't give a shit that little stones dug into my knees; I pawed at his trousers until I got the button unfastened and his zip pulled down, groaning as his cock sprang free. "Are you ... going commando, my Sexy Sir?"

Dean laughed, pushing the hood off my head so he could sink his fingers into my thick curls. "I had plans for us tonight, little slut, but then you tripped my alarms when you broke out and I had to come hunt you."

Ohhhhh, there *had* been enchantments on the gates. Whoops.

I gripped the base of his cock and licked around the head, listening to his breath catch. "I bet you liked hunting me."

"Loved it," he rasped. "I kept picturing what I'd do when I caught you."

I sucked the underside of his cock, flattening my tongue to the vein that curved there and grinning as he jolted in my hand. "And what did you plan to do?" I asked breathily, sucking his thick head into my mouth.

"This," he replied, low and rumbling. "Exactly this, babygirl, but much, much rougher."

I pulled my mouth off his cock with a pop and gave him an unhappy glare from the ground. "And now you're holding back? Just because I'm not running away? How is that fair?"

Dean frowned, caressing the back of my head with his thumb. "I don't want to punish you anymore; you're a good girl, a perfect little killer for me. You deserve only pleasure."

I pouted. "But what if I want you to stop holding back? What if I want everything you have to give me?"

The look he gave me was laced with reproach. "*Everything* will hurt, Rebel. Possibly a lot."

I nodded eagerly, running my hands up his legs, squeezing his thighs and ducking forward to kiss the bobbing tip of his cock. "I don't mind if it hurts, sir. I want all of you, all your dominance and brutality."

A chill skated down my spine at the low, menacing laugh that built in his chest. His hands tightened painfully in my hair, shooting shivers and pleasant sensations down my spine. "Then my perfect little slut will get *everything*. Open your mouth, tongue out; I don't need you to suck when I can use your mouth."

My pussy squeezed, even my ass throbbing, and I relaxed my jaw, letting my tongue loll out of my mouth as he pushed his cock inside—and kept pushing, and *kept* pushing, until my stomach cramped and I gagged.

"Thaaat's it," he breathed, holding my head down with both hands. "Is your belly cramping, babygirl?"

I nodded, as much as I could while my mouth was impaled on his cock, his tip nudging my throat.

"Good," he said harshly, and held me in place until my head went dizzy, until my lungs fought for air, until I started to panic. My stomach spasmed badly, my choking, squelching sounds loud in the quiet night. "I don't care what hurts you, little slut. I only care what feels good to me. Nod if you understand."

True fear started to grip me as my lungs squeezed tighter, the tiny puffs of air I dragged through my nose nowhere near enough. He tightened his grip on my hair and pulled me off his cock, letting me gulp down cold air in loud, desperate gasps. His cock jumped in front of my face with every needy inhale I made, and my hands flattened to his knees for stability as the world blurred and spun around me.

I laid my head against his thigh, panting, half surprised he let me pause there as I caught my breath.

"Pick a safe word, babygirl," he said, wrapping my hair around his wrist. A shiver went down my spine and my clit ached fiercely. *Fuck* yes. Dangerous, threatening, dominant, *and* considerate of my safety? Now I was definitely swooning.

"Unicorn," I said, tipping my head back to stare dazedly as Dean looked down at me, a satisfied smile on his face and cruelty shining from his whiskey eyes, the first hint of the crazed killer who needed to kill and mutilate. What had driven him to this life? None of us ended up here just for the fun of it, even if it *was* fun. There was always a breaking point, a moment when the old you snapped and the new, twisted you took their place.

"Unicorn," he agreed with a little laugh, keeping one hand wrapped up in my hair and gripping my chin with the other. "If you can't talk and you need to stop, you hit my thighs, okay?"

I nodded, blurry and confused in the best way. And I could breathe again now; I wanted more of the gruff sounds he made while I choked on him, wanted the ruthless voice that replied *good* when I told him it hurt. I was so wet my underwear was soaked through, my jeans probably sporting a wet patch too.

"Tongue out, little slut. I want to feel it against my balls when I fuck your whore mouth."

I shuddered at the degradation, my toes curling in my boots. And that was before he slapped me for taking too long to respond. It was light enough to not hurt, to not even make my face burn, but abrupt enough to shock me. I'd never even liked slapping before, but something about Dean made it so fucking hot.

I opened my mouth, my tongue hanging out, and Dean rumbled in satisfaction, staring down at me with blazing brown eyes. "That's my good fucking toy."

Ohhhhh, that name made pleasure squeeze my pussy deep, my body tingly and hot. I wanted him to touch me so badly, but his grip on my hair was hot too, and I'd asked for every bit of his dominance. I'd take every single thing he had to give me.

I relaxed my mouth and throat as he thrust in, shallow at first, letting me get used to the rough, rapid movements. The feel of his thick veiny cock sliding over my tongue made my hips writhe against air, desperate for touch.

"Stay still," he commanded in that vicious voice that sent genuine chills through me. I could believe this man was a serial killer, and one cold and calculated enough to only kill once a year. *My* serial killer—mine. All fucking mine. I flicked my tongue against his cock, hollowing my cheeks and sucking him greedily, aching to show him how much I loved that he was mine, how much I loved his bloody alter ego.

"I said—" he snapped, ripping me off his cock and using his grip on my hair to shake my head so my brains rattled in my skull.

Ooh, woahhhhh, the alleyway was spinning like a merry-go-round. Drool and saliva dripped in a messy line down the front of my hoodie, but I barely noticed.

"—stay fucking still," he finished, so cold and deadly that I whimpered. Not for him to stop, but to give me *more*. "If I wanted a cocksucker, I'd have found another slut."

I growled at that, the sound coming from deep within my chest, so full and loud I shocked myself.

His huff of a laugh had me looking up at him, and the smug male smirk on his face drove me wild. I half wanted to slap it from his lips, half wanted to rip my clothes off and offer him my pussy there on the floor. "I hear you, babygirl," he said, his eyes intense in a different way than before. "You can stop growling now."

"You're mine," I snarled, glaring up at him. "This cock is *mine,* only mine."

His eyes flashed vivid gold and he grabbed my head, holding me still while his hips snapped forward, fucking my mouth with wild, animal need. I gagged as he hit the back of my throat, my eyes watering, but he didn't give me time to get used to it this time, using me roughly.

Pleasant tingles rushed down my back as he tightened his grip on my hair, using it to pull my mouth up and down his cock, a rough grunt leaving his throat every time he filled my mouth. I hadn't forgotten his earlier remark; even as I gasped and choked, I stretched out my tongue, wiggling it against the underside of his cock. I wanted my alpha to lose control, wanted to drive him mad.

"Yess," he said roughly, his loud grunt filling the tight alleyway. "But you can do better than that, Miss Falcon. I know you can take me deeper."

I whimpered as he withdrew—and immediately plunged back into my mouth. My body seized with the force of my stomach cramp, my hands fluttering around his thighs, but I panted through my nose and didn't tap out. Yet.

"Fuck." His grip on my hair tightened as I flicked the tip of my tongue over his balls, a rush of accomplishment filling me as he choked on a groan. It was the hottest sound I'd ever heard, and I wanted more.[6] "Fuck, like that, stay right there and lick my balls."

I tried to obey him, reaching out my tongue to lick further, but the demand for air made my lungs burn, and my stomach twisted so hard I was sure I'd be sick. I tapped frantically at his thighs, and when he released me, I dragged gulping breaths of biting air into my lungs, my whole body covered in goosebumps.

"You tried, at least," he said in a patronising tone that should have turned me all the way off.[7]

My lungs hurt, every breath I dragged in seemed to scrape them raw, and don't even get me started on how sore my throat was. But getting my sexy sir to let go and give himself over to the killer darkness he kept hidden was worth it. And I'd make sure he pampered me with care, affection, and a dozen cups of soothing peppermint tea when we got back to Blake Hall.

"On your feet, little slut," he commanded, releasing his tight fist on my hair as I wobbled to my feet and he steadied me with a solid grip on my hip.

"Look at the mess you made," he said, but he made it sound like a good thing, his whiskey eyes bright with intent. The front of my hoodie was definitely messy, but that was what you got when a crazy dominant alpha fucked your throat. Nobody ever said sex was clean and tidy, and if they did, they were lying. "Better take that off, hmm?"

A deep throb went through my pussy at his low voice, at the tone. When I stopped being so disoriented, I unzipped my hoodie and threw it to the floor, not really caring about the cold when his rough hands covered my body. The thin straps of my vest got pushed down my arms until the fabric gathered around my waist, baring the cute pink bra I was wearing.

"Very pretty," he murmured, his big hands spanning the width of my waist, burning hot where I was chilled.

"Thank you," I replied with a beaming grin. I squeaked when he grabbed the lacy cups and tore them apart, throwing my bra aside like it was rubbish. "Hey! That was one of my favourites. You better buy me a new—oh!"

He tugged on my nipples until I was flush to his body, my naked chest against his jacket sooooo fucking hot. I felt dirty and exposed and I *loved* it because I knew I was safe with Dean. He wouldn't let anyone see me.

"Less attitude please, Miss Falcon." When I kept my lips pressed shut to show him I could obey, a satisfied smile crossed his face. "Better. I knew you could be good for me." He rolled my nipples between his fingers, his stare fixed on my face as need boiled up between my legs. "Remember what I told you?"

"Umm..." He'd told me a lot.

He laughed, a deep, callous sound, and backed me up against the wall. I gasped at the hard, freezing stone, and swore his eyes turned a shade darker.

"This will hurt," he reminded me, releasing my nipples to unfasten my jeans and yank them over my thighs. "*No*," he said firmly as I shifted to move them lower. "Keep them where they are. You don't need freedom of movement for this."

Oh, fuckkkk. Was I panting like a bitch in heat? I was panting like a bitch in heat.

I'd never been with someone this dominant before, never been controlled so entirely, never submitted fully like this. I'd *thought* I'd had good sex before, but whoa, this was something else.

"You better be wet," he rumbled, grabbing my hips and spinning me so suddenly that the world tipped and I giggled. My hands snapped out on instinct, saving me a broken nose and missing front teeth, and I'd just managed to spread my palms across the stone when Dean grabbed my ass and impaled me on his cock.

I shouted out, so loud that someone must have heard, but he didn't silence me; he laughed with wicked pleasure, forcing me into the wall with rough, unyielding thrusts.

"Is this what you wanted?" he demanded with so much alphaness in his voice that I wilted against the wall with a whimper. "You wanted me to fuck this pussy? You wanted me to use you like a ragdoll, like a toy? *Well?*"

"Yes," I choked out, my eyes squeezed shut as he took me so hard and fast that I couldn't process the sensations exploding through me. I started to shake, my pussy tightening on his cock, and my breaths coming in shattered pants.

"You wanted a vicious killer to make you his broken doll?" he demanded, his palm coming down in a sharp spank against my ass.

My toes curled, and all I could do was whimper.

"Answer me, or you don't get to come."

"Yes!" I cried. "Yes, that's what I wanted, and I fucking love it!" Words bubbled up and spilled out as his palm smacked my other cheek, and then the other again. His spanks were so fast that I couldn't process the burn, couldn't tell if it was pleasure or pain as he slammed deeper inside me, his hips right against my stinging backside. It was overwhelming and dizzying, like hanging upside down from a rollercoaster, adrenaline thumping through every part of me, and my pussy clenched sporadically, climax so fucking close.

"Dirty fucking slut," he snarled, grabbing a fistful of my hair and wrenching my neck back. My mouth fell open at this new angle, a wordless cry ripping out of my throat. "You *love* this? You love being fucked so much it hurts by a man who's killed seven people? You love being touched by hands that have been drenched in blood?"

"Fuck!" I screamed, and came so hard it was like a detonation. It was a good thing Dean was gripping my hip and my hair because I collapsed into violent spasms, my body jerking and my pussy locked tight around his ruthless cock.

When I floated back to earth, my skull stung fiercely, and various points on my body throbbed with pain—my pussy equally brutalised by his roughness—but that faded into the background for now as Dean buried himself to the hilt and growled, so loud the residents of this quaint little village must have thought a lion had got loose.

His cock jolted inside me as he came, making my body shake again as he tilted my head further back and sank his sharp canines into the same spot he'd bitten before. Aftershocks rocked my pussy, my eyes wide at the force of them.

"Wow," I gasped, shivering as Dean's fingers loosened in my hair, running gently through the long curls.

"Mm," he agreed, his other hand sliding around my front to cup my breast. "You were perfect."

I leant back against him, melting inside. He kept calling me that; he must have really meant it.

"Are you hurt, babygirl?" he asked, the sinister edge in his voice softened until he was my protective alpha again.

"A little," I admitted, my breaths evening out as my body finally went limp and relaxed. His gentle touches felt as good as his rough treatment, and I was one lucky girl to get both.

"I shouldn't love that as much as I do," he said with a husky laugh.

"That's my life motto," I replied with a snicker, finally opening my eyes and returning to reality. To a freezing, dark pathway and my jeans shoved around my knees, and my vest pulled down so my tits pebbled in the cold. And Dean's cock still buried inside me, softening as fluids leaked down my thigh. And nowhere nearby for us to shower. Ick.

Dean's tongue swirled over the bite he'd opened up again, the tether between us swelling with affection. He finally withdrew his cock, careful not to hurt me this time, and retrieved my hoodie while I pulled up my jeans and tucked my boobs into my vest. My poor bra! I pouted as he put it in his pocket, no ruefulness in his eyes, just satisfaction.

"I'll buy you another," he promised, hooking his arm around my waist and bringing me in for a deep, passionate kiss.

"You better," I warned against his lips, running my fingers over his short, scratchy beard, and through his silver hair. "Or no more sexytimes for you, my Straw Man."

"Fuck," he growled, dragging me back to his lips for a deep, devouring kiss, nipping my bottom lip. "It makes me so hot hearing you call me that, Graves. Wait." He straightened, his eyes sharpening. "Edison Bray knows who you are;

he called you that before you attacked him. I didn't realise the significance at the time."

"Yeah…" I slipped out of his arms and hunted down my murder bag where it had ended up slung on the ground. "Let's not talk about Edison, shall we?"

Dean was quiet for so long that I was forced to glance back at him, and a chill tripped down my spine at the look in his eyes—like he was planning to disembowel someone. Slowly.

"You can't kill him," I sighed, zipping my hoodie up. "He's my mate. Sort of. He rejected me."

I jolted at Dean's deafening growl, and then he was in front of me, his hot hands cupping my face as his lip curled back from his deadly teeth. "He did *what?*"

I shrugged, as if it didn't hurt like hell. "He's an heir to his family, I'm a dud, it's fine. I'm over it."

He surprised me by pressing a soft, lingering kiss to my forehead. "I'll never reject you, babygirl. And neither will anyone who matters. I promise you."

It was a raw, bleeding wound that had never sealed over, but Dean's words eased the pain a fraction. "You're very sweet for a serial killer. Anyone ever tell you that, Sexy Sir?"

Dean laughed. "I can't say they have, Miss Falcon." He laid another kiss, this time on my cheek. "Let's go back to the hall. I can plan what I'm going to do to Bray back there."

"Nothing. You're going to do nothing to Bray."

He didn't reply, just linked his fingers with mine, took my bag and slung it over his own shoulder, and led me out of the alleyway.

"Right?" I pressed.

"Right, Dean?"

He didn't answer.

15

"Do I *have* to?" I whined, giving Dean my best pleading look as he put away the enchanted key that had transported us here. To the edge of a scary high ravine surrounded by an open sky filled with fluffy clouds. A forest stretched away at our backs, and ahead, five perilous rope bridges spanned the mile-long distance to the other side of the ravine. "Can I not and say I did?" I made my eyes extra big and pleading. It didn't hurt that my voice was a little scratchy, even after the honey and lemon he'd made for my throat, reminding him of our hot as hell alley sex. "I'll suck your cock to sweeten the deal."

"Slut," one of the other trialists coughed under his breath—one of the wolves. The rangy one with the goatee. Frank.

"*What* did you just call my mate?" Dean growled, instantly menacing.

Goatee Dick went pale.

I took three steps, grabbed Goatee's shoulders, and pushed. I danced back as he tipped over the edge, his arms pinwheeling at his sides. "Oops," I deadpanned, meeting the eyes of every single trialist as Goatee's screams faded into silence far below. "He slipped."

"That's breaking the rules," Boyband hissed, baring his fangs. "We're not allowed to harm any of the others while taking the trials."

"Correct," Dean replied, still harsh and growly. "While on the bridge, you're forbidden to attack each other. But you haven't begun your trial yet, have you?"[1]

I gave Boyband a smug little smile, reaching into my hoodie pocket for a lollipop and unwrapping it noisily. "What?" I asked when I found them all staring at me. "It's a long bridge; I need my sustenance."

Dean laughed, a low rumbly sound that made me shiver. Brunel and Vom, the other wolves, smartly averted their eyes, while Boyband watched on in boredom.

"Go on then," Dean ordered. "The sooner you cross your bridge, the sooner you can go back to the hall. And the sooner I don't have to be babysitting you bastards," he muttered. "I'll follow the edge and meet you on the other side."

No time limit on this trial? That was good. I'd never been terrified of heights, but something about dangling on a bit of rope and wood over deadly rapids made me nervous.[2] Rushing it would only get me a spot on the river bed next to Goatee.

"No," he growled as the big, burly wolf stepped towards the furthest bridge. "You each have your own. Brunel, that's yours. Vom, you're next in line. Miss Falcon, yours is the one after that."

"They look exactly the same," I pointed out, pushing my lollipop into my cheek so I could speak. Dean's eyes darkened to liquid amber and I smirked. Oops. Apparently the bulge in my cheek was making him think of other things. I pulled the sweet from my mouth with a swirling lick I made sure he saw every moment of. "Why do we need our own?"

"So there's no cheating and it's fair," he replied, an octave lower. "Now stop stalling, and start your trial. Wilson, you're on the end."

Ehh, I was still going to call him Boyband.

"See you on the other side, Sexy Sir!" I said and ignored the faint snickers from our audience as I skipped onto the rope bridge—and immediately slowed down, my stomach dropping waaaayyy below. Shit, that was far. If I wasn't careful, I'd break my neck and splatter on the rocks poking out of the white, frothing water below.

"Okay, Rebel," I said under my breath, discarding my lolly and gripping the ropes on either side of the narrow slats as I took careful steps. "You're a badass assassin lady. You can do this."

Knowing Dean would be waiting on the other side helped, but there was no ignoring the roaring water below, so loud it drowned out anything Brunel, Vom, and Boyband were saying on either side of me. I kept my feet moving steadily and my eyes fixed down, watching where I placed them. The rope chafed at my palms, but I refused to let go even when it broke skin. It was the only thing I had to hold onto, and I might have been able to kill a man with my bare thighs, but I didn't trust my balance right now.

"Okay," I breathed. "Nearly there now."

I glanced up to see if my guess was correct and my shoulders slumped. I wasn't even a quarter of the way across, and I must have been walking for twenty minutes now. At least. This was going to take forever.

I let myself whine and complain as I crossed the next section of planks, the water churning so high it splashed the slats and made each step perilous.

"Don't fall, Rebel," I breathed, clutching the ropes. "Just don't fall. That's all you have to do. If these wolf morons can do it, so can you."

But my foot slid out from under me on my next step, and I shrieked, tightening my fingers into fists around the guide ropes as I wobbled precariously, the water rushing and roaring below, like a monster eager to eat me.

"Okay," I gasped. "Okay, I'm okay."

I steadied, clutching the ropes in a chokehold as I caught my breath, my legs like jelly. How was this supposed to prove I was a worthy paranormal who wouldn't go off on a magic-fuelled murder spree? This was more like a deadly Duke of Edinburgh award, and I didn't like it one bit.

But I steadied on the slick boards, and when I started breathing again, I took slow steps, refusing to look anywhere but forward, at the jagged spit of land where Dean would be waiting. Where *solid ground* waited.

"Almost there," I breathed, the lie sour on my tongue.

I made it halfway, but breathing was difficult and I was so tense my shoulders might be permanently locked around my neck. My hair was plastered to my cheeks and the back of my neck with sweat and water, and the ropes had grown slick under my palms. Boyband was already across, which didn't seem fair considering his speed advantage, but I didn't know if the wolves were keeping pace with me or if they'd fallen off. With the water rushing this loud, I wouldn't hear their screams.

The sun shifted in the sky, burning the back of my neck, but I was so close to the end now, the posts jutting up from the scraggly grass luring me in like a siren call.

"Almost there," I panted, and it wasn't a lie this time. "Almost—"

A scream cut off my words as the next two boards

collapsed beneath my weight, and air whipped past my face sharp enough to cut. I scrabbled at the planks as my lower half crashed through the bridge and dangled dangerously, but the edges were damp with water and sanded smooth so I couldn't even dig my nails in.

Wait … sanded?

The last thought I had before I plummeted into the rapids was that there should have been *jagged* edges. Someone had purposefully cut my bridge; someone wanted me to fail this trial.

Someone was trying to kill me.

16

*I*f I'd been thinking, I would have sucked in a deep breath before my body struck the violent water. But I couldn't stop screaming as I fell, the fall terrifying and dizzying in a way I'd never experienced before, and thinking was impossible. My hair wrapped around my face, water splashed into my eyes, and I couldn't *see*, couldn't tell if I was up or down until I slammed into a solid weight.

It took me a disoriented second to realise the brick wall I'd crashed into was the water, and my entire chest and shoulder was bruised, flashing with pain. I was smart enough to slam my mouth shut and conserve air now, but it was too little, too late. And I'd never been a strong swimmer.

I kicked my feet, pumping my arms, but the water was moving too fast, spinning me up, down, and in every fucking direction like I was a teddy bear in a washing machine.

My brain shook inside my skull until I couldn't think, and only instinct kept my arms flailing and legs kicking. Where the fuck was *up*? Where was the surface? I spun and fell through the water, squinting my eyes open to see nothing but thrashing darkness. There were rocks in here, right? Dangerous, knifey ones that could cut me open? I could be whirling straight for one, and I'd never know.

My lungs burned fiercely, a thousand times worse than when Dean choked me on his cock, and I didn't have anyone to pull me back, to stroke my face and praise me now. There was only certain death, suffocation, and bubbles of water shoving themselves up my nose until I was choking, spinning wildly.

A huge ripple went through the water, thrashing me to the side, and I screamed using the last of my air when my shoulder rammed into a sharp rock, the joint knocked out of alignment. It wasn't the first time I'd had my shoulder dislocated but *fuckkkkk*, it hurt.

Water rushed around me—no *towards* me—and then parted as a huge shadow reached for me.

I whimpered, wondering if I was seeing things, half waiting for a shark to open huge jaws and swallow me whole. But instead, a hand closed around my good arm, big enough to dwarf my shoulder, and I was tugged upwards in a dizzying, blurring rush. Black spots crowded into my vision, a vicious pain cut my chest as my lungs demanded air, and I stupidly inhaled through my nose, instinct fighting intelligence.

But then I was *out* of the water, with air scalding my freezing skin and the hardness of the riverbank slamming into my stomach. I couldn't hear anything but rushing water, couldn't see anything but blurs as I retched.

A rough hand pushed my shoulder back into place and slammed me on the back, and I shrank away as a massive shadow blotted out the sun. "Cough, little scorpion," a low, thunderous voice said, so deep it was more vibration than sound. "Cough it up."

I followed his advice and the urging of the slams against

my back, coughing and vomiting water and bile, making a pitiful moan of pain when it stopped. My body ached *everywhere*, like I'd been run through a blender, and his rough smacks hadn't helped. The man was built like a fucking tank.

"S...stalker?" I rasped, trying to blink the stinging water out of my eyes. "That you?"

"You're cold," he rumbled, and a body twice the size of my own pressed to my back, tugging me against a barrel chest as arms wrapped around my middle.

"Pretty ... forward," I remarked, but a wave of reassurance hit me strong enough to make me wilt, and I tilted my head back against a shoulder made of hard muscle, still shook by the occasional cough. "Mate?"

"Mate," he agreed, gravelly yet soft. I shuddered as his scorching hot hand trailed up and down my thigh. He didn't seem to care that my jeans were drenched, but then he'd dived in to rescue me; he was as soaked as I was. "Can you breathe now?"

"Just about," I replied, but my head was still whirling like I was trapped in the deadly thrash of the rapids. Every part of me hurt, and I was *not* looking forward to the walk up to the ravine top. At least we could use Dean's witch charm to get back to Blake Hall. Wait... "You followed us here. How? We came by charm."

Sluggish, I twisted around to look at my behemoth of a stalker, and my eyes widened. Wet black hair clung to the roughly carved planes of his forehead, cheeks, and jaw, and the entire right side of his face, neck, and shoulder rippled with burn scarring, fiercely red against the alabaster of his unmarred skin. But it was the way his gaze dropped before I could see the colour of his irises that caught and held my attention, and the way his mouth tugged down, his shoulders slumping to follow the movement.

He avoided my gaze, but didn't let go, didn't move at all, actually. Like he was waiting for something. The lowered eyes, the way he'd gone still ... all signs of submission. Like *I* was the bigger predator when he was six-foot-*a-lot*, broad shouldered, barrel chested, and had hands the size of freaking dinner plates. "I have this," he replied quietly, and moved with exaggeratedly slow movements to point out the bee pin on his chest.

"Ah," I replied, not staring at the way his wet T-shirt clung to his huge pectoral muscles, or fell into the dips of his six pack, accentuating muscles that took a hell of a lot of work to keep up. *Definitely* not staring. Me? Stare with glazed eyes? Drool gathering in my mouth? No, ma'am.

"I will not hurt you," he said without prompting, his voice little more than a raspy whisper, sharply accented with something clearly of Eastern European origin. He gave me super hot bodyguard vibes. Ooh! Maybe he was a bond villain planning the timely demise of a gag-worthy do-gooder.[1]

I dragged my gaze from his mouth-watering chest,[2] a furrow scrunching my brows. "Huh? Why would you hurt me; you're my mate, dummy." I could feel the bond, but only faintly. Every time I reached out to it, it rushed away like a skittish creature.

A matching frown drew his thick brows together, and I turned around fully to meet his gaze, making a *blech* sound at all the sodden material clinging to me, slapping the grassy rocks when I sat back. My stalker was a damned gentleman; his gaze didn't dip once to my boobs, even though my nipples were standing out like a stripper in a nunnery. My hoodie must have come unzipped in the washing machine nightmare that was the rapids, and my shirt hugged my body every bit as thirstily as the behemoth's clothing did.

"Most people," he replied slowly, like he was choosing the right words, "think I kill them."

I tilted my head. "Do you? Kill people? I know that's normally a bad thing," I added in a rush, my voice sore and husky thanks to my drowning escapade, "but I'm not against a teeny bit of killing, myself. So if you *did* hurt people, I wouldn't judge."

"I don't mean to," he said quietly, and I sighed in sympathy, my heart going all achy and sad. "Once," he added, his gaze fixed squarely on the rapids still noisily rushing past us, throwing foam and water onto the bank. "That's why I'm here."

"On a riverbank soaking through to your underwear?" I asked, hoping he'd laugh. His moroseness was making my insides hurt. I wanted to hear his laugh, to see what his smile looked like, to know if it filled his cheeks or was just a tiny curve in the corner of his mouth.

He huffed a laugh, but didn't smile, and said again, "I won't hurt you."

"I know, big guy," I assured him, patting his shoulder before I climbed to my feet, almost stumbling under the weight of my soaked clothes. At least my shoulder didn't hurt anymore. "Don't worry, I can handle myself. You wouldn't be able to hurt me if you tried."

At that, he sagged in relief, and followed my lead as he stood, grabbing the thighs of his jeans and wringing the water out of them. My mouth popped open as the thick outline of his cock pushed against the tight, wet fabric, and my body went hot all over. Holy kittens, that was a big cock. Enormous. But why was I surprised when the rest of him was massive? He could honestly snap my neck in a second with those huge hands, and yet all he'd done was save me, and promise not to hurt me.

I watched him wring the water out of his clothes with a frown. The way he'd stalked me through the whimpering woods, and then grabbed me in Blake Hall's foyer made me think he was dangerous and maybe a little bit evil. But now I wasn't so sure. Now I was wondering if his rough, bruising grip hadn't been dominance, but because he had no idea how strong he was.

I don't mean to.

My heart went to mush, and by the time he was finished wringing out his clothes, I was staring at him like he was a terminally ill puppy.

"What?" he asked, his voice so deep and gravelly I *felt* it moving through me. "You watch me. Why?"

And now I was looking at him like he was a teeny tiny kitten trying to leap onto a huge sofa. He was so CUTE, with his wide eyes—yellowish green now I could get a proper look at him—and his hunched shoulders and his faltering English. I wanted to bundle him into a handbag and carry him around with me everywhere like a Chihuahua.[3] "I like watching you," I replied, trying for cute and sultry. But I didn't feel cute and sultry, I felt battered and drowned and pitiful. But hey, maybe that was his type?

A deeper furrow formed between his brows, his frown tugging down his burn scars. "You're lying," he said, and didn't sound surprised.[4] "We walk now. That way."

He pointed at the row of rangy trees I hadn't even noticed behind us, and set off, trudging past me and towards a thin path.

"I don't even know your name, big guy," I said, hurrying

to catch up with his massive strides. "Can you slow down? Some of us don't have Amazon-ish legs."

He stopped in the middle of the path, and I nearly tumbled into him, catching myself at the last second and wincing at the stinging ache that went through my knees. Had I hit them on something? I couldn't remember, but they hurt like *hell*. "Like the website?" he asked with a deep frown, confusion darkening his olive eyes.

"What?" I asked, tipping my head back, back, back until I met his eyes. Mmmmm, he was tall. I barely came up to the middle of his chest, and the size difference was putting all sorts of ideas in my head. But he'd been nothing but gentlemanly to me, and he hadn't looked at my tits once, so maybe he wasn't attracted to me. That thought hurt deep, but I breathed around it, took it into me like all the other pains in my body, and smiled like that smile could chase off the hurt. The least I could do in repayment for him saving my life was not ogle him like the human personification of the male gaze.

"Amazon," he replied, his confusion clear.

"Oh!" I brightened, giving him a big grin. "Well, it's a place too, like a massive rainforest, and also these people from mythology who are super tall and epic fighters and just really cool. Not the temperature—"

"I know cool," he cut in, intelligence spinning behind his deep-set eyes. "Amazon. Tall fighters. Rainy forest." He nodded, already turning back onto the path—but he walked slower, letting me catch up. "Thank you."

"For what?" I peeled my wet shirt off my stomach and followed his example, wringing the water out of it as we walked into the sparse tree cover. I scowled up at the bright sun; the last thing I needed when I was wet and in pain was to be burned.

"Teaching," he replied, ducking his head to avoid my gaze again. "I can't knowing everything. But I want to."

I blinked, a piece of the puzzle that was my behemoth stalker sliding into place; he was eager to learn, and curious about everything. Probably a perfectionist, too. "Well, you're welcome, big guy." I reached up to pat his shoulder and resisted the urge to squeeze all that muscle that was *right there*, begging for me to massage it.

"Hugh Petrov," he said after another few steps, as birds rustled leaves and tweeted high above us, answering the question I'd asked a while back.

"*Huge* Petrov?" I asked, trying not to choke. Damn, he was aptly named.

"Hugh," he repeated, but there was a richness and rumbly quality to his voice that suggested amusement.

"Ohhhhhhh, *Hugh* Petrov," I laughed, peering up at him and delighted when he met my eyes with a brazen gaze. "Well, it's nice to meet you, Hugh. I'm Rebel Falcon." I struck my hand out sideways for him to shake while we walked, and couldn't fight a body-wide shudder as his hot hand dwarfed my own. It felt soooooo good. Too good. He showed no signs of wanting me, I reminded myself, and ignored the hurt that stabbed deeper.

"Falcon?" He shook his head, long black hair flinging drops of water into his face. "No. You're a scorpion." He watched me from the corner of his eye as we ducked under a low branch,[5] something like warmth in his voice as he said, "You're deadly. Beautiful."

My whole body went hot. Okay, maybe he had noticed me after all.

"Still... still..." He scowled, a rush of sharp, fluid words coming from deep in his chest. I was swooning, head over heels for whatever he'd just said in his native language until he added in English, "Still can be killed. You slipped?"

"Hmm?" I shook myself. He was right. I *could* be killed, and someone had tried to kill me. "No, someone sabotaged my fucking bridge. They cut the slats so I'd fall."

A low, rattling growl filled the space around us, echoing off the tall trees until a dozen vicious wolves roared in rage. I stopped dead, my eyes wide as instincts fired off inside me, my new wolf side warring with my mate instincts, fear versus logic. He wouldn't hurt me, couldn't actually hurt me, but damnnnnnn he was alpha as hell. Was he ... more alpha than Dean? I'd thought he was submissive and sweet, but maybe that was just to me?

"What is sabotaged?" he demanded, so low the words were barely audible.

My knees went weak. "Making sure someone fucks up. Wrecking someone's chances on purpose. Messing with a bridge so someone falls off it before they can reach the end."

I wasn't sure which part made sense to him, but understanding flashed in his eyes, and his previous alpha growl was just the warm up. This one sent me to my knees on the dirty ground, my cheek pressed to the hard ground and my backside thrust up in the air, wiggling from side to side.

Ah.

Maybe ... um. Maybe his growl didn't terrify my inner wolf; maybe it made her horny. Because I was *presenting* to him, wiggling my backside to entice him like I was a bitch in heat.

His growl deepened in timbre, not so much a roar as a pleasant vibration. I didn't understand a word of his reply because it was in Polish or Russian or whatever his language actually was. But I recognised the tone—soft and sensual. His giant hand slid over my ass, the wet jeans moulded to my shape, and I jolted as his thumb dipped lower to rub over my pussy as he squeezed my ass.

"You make very pretty picture, little scorpion," he said, with a rumble so damn close to a purr. I shuddered, pushing back against his hand and gasping as his thumb slid to my clit. He pressed down hard, finding it as if he instinctively knew where would give me the most pleasure. Maybe he did? Maybe it was part of the mate starter kit. Windows laptops came with Microsoft Office. Mates came with Extra-Accurate Clit Location.[6] "Is this show for me?"

I nodded, swallowing a moan as he circled his thumb, the friction through my jeans enough to push me halfway to orgasm with only a few swipes. "For you. *Fuck*, Hugh."

He knelt behind me, arching over me to press a hot, lingering kiss to the back of my neck. "Is this kitty for me, too?"

I smiled at his wrong word use. Although language was made up nonsense that humans invented; who was to say kitty wasn't the right word? "Yes," I gasped as he squeezed my other ass cheek with a gentleness that must have taken effort from a man so strong, his thumb still circling over my clit, his pace almost lazy.

"I will ... treasure it," he breathed, his breath hot on the back of my neck. "And you." He sounded a little stunned, like he couldn't believe this was happening. How many people had taken one look at him and thought he was a big, bad guy? I had, too, but that was never a bad thing to me. But to most people...

"I'll treasure you, too," I gasped out, heat twisting tighter in my lower belly. I dug my fingers into the dirt, rolling my hips against his hands. "I treasure all my mates."

He shuddered above me, clutching my ass harder. "Even me?"

"Especially you," I choked out. "Fuck, keep doing that."

"I won't stop," he promised. "This is gift you give me, little scorpion. I love feeling you under me."

That last part sent me over the edge, and I gasped and bucked under him, my pussy clenching

"Beautiful," he praised, dragging another deep throb from my clit. "But we need walk again. Wet clothes are bad."

"Mm," I agreed, flopping onto the ground and rolling over so I could reach up and grasp his face. "Definitely bad." But I tugged him down for a kiss. His lips pressed sweetly against my lips before drawing back. Awww, he didn't even try to maul my mouth like my other guys did. Hugh was a teddy bear. "*My* big teddy bear," I murmured, and nuzzled his jaw before he moved away, getting to his feet and offering a hand to help me up.

"Come on, little scorpion," he said, all warm and deep. "Let's get dry. And find others."

I winced. Dean was not going to be happy when he learned someone had tried to kill me. I wondered if the papers might end up splashed with another Straw Man murder soon.

17

I shivered, still cold in my bones after a scorching hot shower back at Blake Hall, and huddled up against Hugh's warmth. My stalker behemoth held me, his big body wrapped around me from behind as we sat on my bed.

"Call him back," Dean growled, pacing a hole in the floor by the door, a vein standing out on his forehead and his alpha-ness making me limp and submissive.

"I can't," I huffed, turning my face to snuggle deeper into my stalker, his scent of woodsy aftershave tickling my nose. "It doesn't work like that; I'm his mate, not his keeper."

"Use the bond," Dean argued, spinning to face me with such a scary expression that my clit throbbed. "Drag him back here."

"No," I replied petulantly, my brows low. Every single part of my body ached, but at least I was comfy and cosy here cuddled up to Hugh. It made my throbbing knee and raw throat easier to bear. "Why should I? He has a right to be angry."

Slasher had taken one look at me, soaking wet,

battered by the water and bruised by the deadly fall, and he'd gone still. Not physically, but inside—I'd felt it, like everything had frozen between us. He'd ducked his head for a swift kiss to my lips, something about the gesture clipped and controlled, and said he'd find who had tried to kill me.

But even my psycho vampire rampaging through Blake Hall's rooms hadn't turned loose the attempted murderer, and Dean stepped in before my Slasher could kill anyone. Anyone *else*, I mean. He'd already ripped the hearts out of two vampires when they tried to restrain him. Oops. With my alpha standing between Slasher and justice, he'd turned to the front door and blurred before anyone could catch him.

That was an hour ago, and no one could find him now. Guards had been dispatched to the village, but it was eerie and silent, no screams or cries for help as a vampire butchered his way through the general populace.

"Whoever he kills is on you, Miss Falcon," Dean rumbled, stalking for the door. His jaw was so tightly clenched I worried it would stay that way.

"That's bullshit. Whoever he kills is on him. I told you; I'm not his keeper, Dean. Would you want me to bring *you* back if you went on a rampage?" I held his gaze, challenging, and saw the truth there, even if he tried to hide it with a scowl. "Exactly," I huffed. "He'll come back when he's ready."

"He might not," Dean muttered, twisting the door handle so roughly I expected it to snap off.

"He will," I insisted, a blare of alarm in my belly. He *would* come back. He wouldn't leave me. "He'd never leave me, I know he wouldn't. He's ... infatuated with me."

Dean grunted.

"I agree," Hugh said, his deep voice making me jump as he stroked my outer thigh. "Slasher will be back."

So. Cute. And so sweet to try to soothe my raw fears. I turned in his arms and cupped his square-jawed, scarred face, kissing him deeply. I was growing to like the smooth ripples of his scars under my fingers—like *a lot*—especially because of the soft growl that vibrated his chest like a purr, making my girly bits fire off like a New Year's fireworks display.

I jumped at the loud slam of my door, and whipped around to find Dean gone. My shoulders sank. It wasn't my fault I had a bunch of sexy, tempting mates. It was destiny's fault. But I didn't like him being jealous and frowny.

"Be right back." I gave Hugh another, deeper kiss and climbed off the bed, shuddering at the loss of his furnace-like heat as I wrapped a heavy cardigan around myself and went after my alpha mate. Although ... I had two very alpha mates now. Maybe that was the problem. Dean hadn't seemed nearly as pissed off when it was just him, me, and Slasher.

"Wait," I called, hurrying across the landing at the top of the foyer steps to catch up to him. "Dean."

He turned only far enough to scowl, but he jerked his head, so I followed him across the hall and into his office. Ooh, desk sex! No, bad Rebel. Now is *not* the time.[1]

"What's going on in your head?" I asked, watching the taut line of his shoulders as he stalked around his desk, threw a bunch of files from his chair onto the floor—not bothering to pick them up when papers splayed out everywhere—and dropped into the seat.

I picked tangles out of my damp, pink curls as I approached his ornate desk, taking a seat in the leather chair and resisting the urge to play with the toggle of the desk lamp like last time. But like a cat with a dangly string, it tempted me to play.

"Dean," I said softly—serious for once. I didn't like the tension on his face or the way he'd closed off, only showing irritation and anger. "What's going on? I thought we were okay."

His mouth pressed thin, and he stared at his tidy desk, his chest heaving.

Oh. Were we *not* okay?

My whole body curled in on itself, and I nodded in reply to what he'd said with his body language if not his words, and I stood, everything inside feeling brittle.

"Sit down, babygirl."

After a brief hesitation, I did, but only because of the ragged tiredness in his voice.

With a rough sigh, running his hand along his stubbled jaw, Dean finally met my gaze. There was so much churning in those whiskey eyes, I couldn't pick out a single emotion. "I'm not mad at you."

I slumped in relief, the teeny-tiniest smile curving the edge of my mouth. "Thank kittens," I breathed. "I thought you were angry I have another mate, and a wolfy alpha at that."

"I'm not thrilled," he growled, his mouth twisting to one side. "But," he added, even growlier, "if he's your mate, I'll accept that. If he makes you happy, good. If he ever upsets you, I'll rip his balls off and feed them to him until he pukes."

I sighed dreamily, even as something inside reared in fury at the threat to my stalker.

"I want to make something clear though, baby," Dean said, arranging the pens on his desk into neat lines. "I don't give a shit if he's used to being the alpha—in this relationship, you are at the top of the fucking hierarchy, and I am right below you. He's the bottom of the ladder." With a smirk, he added, "Until you claim another mate."

"I didn't mean to claim this one," I whined, scratching at the green leather of the seat beneath me. "It's not like I planned it. But he saved me, and he's so sweet and protective and—I like him."

"He better like you, too," Dean replied in a low rumble, his eyes flashing dangerously.

"Or you'll feed him his balls?" I asked with a growing smile.

"Precisely. Now get over here, babygirl. You scared the shit out of me when you fell off that bridge. I was just getting ready to dive in after you when you turned up with Petrov in tow."

I jumped out of my chair and plopped down in his lap, wiggling to get comfy before I wrapped my arms around his neck. "You were going to jump in and save me?"

"I would have," he confirmed, tucking a strand of hair behind my ear.

"I thought dogs hated water, though," I teased, watching his brown eyes darken with intent.

"That's cats you're thinking of, Miss Falcon," he replied, all dangerous and growly. "And wolves are *far* superior to dogs. I'm tempted to think you're trying to insult me." He snapped his teeth, and I squeaked, my heart leaping into a sprint. "Or are you trying to provoke me?" His hand slid down my back and squeezed my ass. "Does my little slut need me to take her over this desk? Remind her that she's mine, and I'll never let anyone hurt her?"

"Yes," I panted, squirming, and—

A swift, light knock sounded on the door, and Dean

swore viciously, pushing me off his lap. "It's Ivelle; I know her knock."

I whined in the back of my throat, but he cut me off by clasping my neck. "Best. Behaviour," he warned, and used his light hold on my throat to lead me back to my seat, pushing me down until my butt met the seat.

"Fine," I huffed, dragging a breath into my lungs to clear the lust and crossing my legs, propping my clasped hands on my knee like I wasn't one touch away from an orgasm.

Dean dropped a kiss on my head and strode for the door. "I'm right in the middle of a session—" he began, but Ivelle strode past him and aimed for me.

She was even cooler up close, little details revealed—her eyes were lined with electric blue makeup the same colour as her braids, her fingernails, earrings, and nose piercing the same blue tone, and the scent of car grease and roses clung to her long coat as she whirled towards me.

"I need to take your statement," she said, making an impatient gesture.

I groaned, but stood, remembering Dean's last order. "I don't know what I can tell you."

"You can give me a list of your enemies for starters," Ivelle huffed, aiming for the door again. "I'll send her back for the rest of your session when I'm done, Dean," emphasising *session* in a way that told us she knew exactly what we'd been about to do. I winced. "And for the record, you don't have to sneak around. With a mate bond in play, you can be open about your relationship."

A pulse of surprise lit up my chest, and I beamed, giving her my best smile.

Dean crossed his arms over his tweed jacket and propped himself against the doorway. "Thanks."

Ivelle nodded, already halfway down the hallway when I next looked at her. "Come on, Rebel."

I scowled, but hurried to catch up after blowing a kiss at my growly mate. "Was anyone else's bridge cut?" I asked, working hard to keep up with Ivelle's long strides, Blake Hall passing in a blur of wood-panelled walls, stale air, and dour paintings.

"No, just yours," she replied, as clipped as her steps.

"I don't have many enemies," I lied. Not many who knew where to find me, anyway. "But I do have a mate who rejected me, who's enrolled or incarcerated here. What's the proper word again?"

She gave me a flatly amused look over her shoulder, heading for a metal spiral staircase. It was decorated with dark stars and moons, denoting her as a witch and the head of the Mystic Club. She was my leader, I guessed. Her and my hippie magic instructor, Vivian, who led the Crescent Club.

"Resident is the correct term," she replied, her steps clomping on the metal staircase as she ascended. I hurried to follow, wondering if she had an idea who might be trying to kill me. I didn't seriously think it was Edison. Although ... what if it was? *Fuck*, that hurt. I even glanced down to see if there was a knife stuck in my chest, but nope, it was just our severed mate bond.

I waved a hand. "Resident, inmate, what's the difference?"

She shot another flat, amused stare at me, reaching for the door handle. The hinges squealed as she shouldered open the old door at the top of the steps, a plume of dust and spiced air exploding. I coughed, dust catching the back of my throat and shoving up my nose, and I waved a hand so I could see in front of me. It had been the same the last time I gave a statement; apparently Ivelle was allergic to dusting.

"Sit," she barked. "I'll open a window."

I tiptoed around the many piles of leather books that formed a precarious, snaking aisle through the high-ceilinged room. I'm sure there were walls somewhere, but I couldn't see them for the books and files towering around me, a small clearing created only for a desk in front of a gothic window. Similarly piled with instruments, defective magical objects, and empty mugs, the desk continued the hoarder theme of the room.

I managed to reach the small circle of empty floor, and sank into the wooden chair before her desk, admiring the phoenixes and unicorns carved into its mahogany legs. Some part of me wanted to reach out and snag a book from the middle of the towers, like a life-sized Jenga game. I bet I could do it without bringing all the piles down. And hell, if I couldn't, the room wouldn't look much different if everything came tumbling down, anyway.

"So, in your own words, tell me about the trial you took today," Ivelle said, lowering into her own seat and reaching back to crank open the warped window. It screaked[2] as badly as the door, but let in blessedly fresh air, clearing out the dust I was choking on.

"I told you, there's not much to tell." My skin itched to have her full focus on me, but I reminded myself I could stab her in a millisecond and my anxiety eased slightly. "I was walking along the bridge like I was meant to, and then the slats fell away under me. They didn't break or snap, they just fell. Someone had cut them, and I know for a fact they'd been sanded; the cut was too smooth. It was intentional—someone tried to kill me." I fixed her with a scowl. "No one was trying to kill me before I came to this place, so it's all your fault. You should really let me go; all the bullshit would stop then."

"Not going to happen," Ivelle replied, unruffled. She leaned back in her chair, watching me unnervingly with blue-ringed dark eyes. "You're a danger to society, and everything we've seen of you this week has only proved that."

I rolled my eyes hard.

"Tell me about Kyle Ladislav," she asked, and I reared back at that name, at the memories of Ana's screams, my locked body, his grunt of satisfaction.

"No," I replied flatly.

"If you want to get out of Blake Hall and back to your life, I need to assess your state of mind."

I couldn't hold back a snort. "Good luck, love. I've had more therapists than I can count, and none of them have been able to do that."

Ivelle held my gaze, weighing, deathly intelligent. "You were a regular citizen until 2017 when you were arrested for the brutal murder of Kyle Ladislav. Did something happen to make you snap, Rebel?"

"You know damn well it did," I growled, some of my wolf side coming out. I could feel the animal writhing inside me, reacting to her cruelty, to those emotions. "You want me to talk about my sister's murder? About how I laid there frozen while she was murdered?"

"Yes," Ivelle replied calmly, taking a pen from a cluttered pot on her desk and hunting for paper.

"No," I replied coldly, and shoved out of the chair. "I'll talk about my feelings when you find whoever's trying to kill me. But I won't hold my breath."

Baring my teeth, I turned my back on her and stalked through the narrow aisle. I paused by the door to viciously kick one of the precarious book towers, and watched in glee as it toppled over, leather spines and yellowed pages clattering to the floor in an explosion of dust.

"Stay out of my business," I warned, and slammed the door to her cluttered office behind myself.

I barely saw the metal staircase as I thundered down it, running mindlessly—just trying to get away.

18

Can't ... breathe...
  Kyle, please...

Ana's pleas were on repeat in my head again, and every memory lashed my heart like a cruel whip, leaving welts that oozed blood. I shook so hard my teeth knocked together, and I didn't bother to look at the hallway stretching in front of me as I stormed down it, my vision laced with tears that turned everything to smudges. Vague blurs suggested windows, doorways, and a coat of armour. Ordinarily, I might have been tempted to wrangle that armour off its stand and try it on for size, but I was about as far from fun and mischievous as I ever got. I'd plummeted into the past so hard, so fast, even killing someone wouldn't soothe this hurt.

I didn't know what I needed, or wanted, or what I would do except keep marching forward and choking on sobs and panting raggedly around the pain in my chest.

"No," I sobbed as I saw the corridor dead-ended in front of me, a sudden end to my frantic path. I had to keep moving, had to outrun my past, my cowardice. Killing Kyle hadn't been enough; I just *laid there* while he killed her. I was as much to blame for her death as he was.

I slammed my fists into the wall, emotion detonating inside me, strong enough to blast me into debris and dust, but the wall swung away under my fists with a quiet creak. A *door*. It was a door, another room, and I sagged in relief. Wiping away the next flow of tears, I rushed through the door, instantly swallowed by a dark space that smelled of paper, ink, and old leather.

I swore to kittens, if I circled back and wound up in Ivelle's office again, I was going to slit her throat and be done with this whole nightmare.

But I knew that wouldn't make me feel better. I was too broken for murder.

Scrubbing at my face, my hitching sobs filling the tall-ceilinged space, I walked cautiously into the room. A library, maybe? I tipped my head back to look at the blurry ceiling and the mezzanine walkway that ringed the hexagonal room beneath a conical roof. Were those golden stars speckling the ceiling? I blinked until I could see clearer, a hush of awe moving through me. Gold leaf accented the wooden beams leading to the ceiling's point, glimmered from the mezzanine, and shone from the stars twinkling on the walls. It was beautiful, and as good a place to collapse into sobs as any.

"Woah, hey," an unwelcome voice breathed—as rich and warm as butter, and ... American? He was clearly startled at the sight of me. Maybe because I was crying. Maybe because I gave off general murder vibes on a daily basis.

"Fuck off," I muttered, not sparing a glance to the figure I saw from the corner of my eye as I walked deeper into the library, heavy wooden shelves keeping the tomes in a kind of order Ivelle's hoard probably envied. I swore each bookshelf was carved from an entire tree, perfuming the dark space with earthy wood. Someone must have spent a long time cleaning this library, because as my eyes focused and my tears dried up, I saw there was no dust anywhere.

I picked a random aisle and stalked down it. Blessed darkness swallowed me, wrapping around me like a cloak as I walked to the furthest end of the little walkway and slid down the wall.

Hide, Rebel.

Quickly, get under the bed...

"Um," that annoying voice intruded on my wallowing and self-torture, and I glared up through teary eyes at the tall, rangy bastard moving tentatively closer. "Tell me I'm butting in where I'm not wanted—"

"You're butting in where you're not—" I snarled, but my voice tangled and lodged in my throat before I could spit the final word. I tried to finish, and again that word choked and died in my throat. "Just fuck off," I growled instead, not caring enough to puzzle out the strangeness of being silenced. Some magic was at play, and it could go fuck itself.

"All right, darling," he murmured, dropping the G so it came out as darlin'. I brought my knees to my chest and gripped them until the bony edges dug into my chest, physical pain echoing the twisted mess of my insides. Thankfully, he didn't hover; he shuffled away, leaving me in suffocating silence with the darkness and weight of the library pressing in around me. It was comforting, that darkness, and I closed my eyes, tilting my head back to soak it in as if the dark were raindrops splattering my face.

I'd always loved darkness, and not just because it was good for hiding bodies. Because it was quiet, and calm, but with the sharp edge of the unknown.

Please...

I flinched. The whimpering woods brought every

memory back to the forefront of my mind. They never really left, but their edges had worn smooth over the years like a pebble wrecked by the sea. Now, the edges were once more sharp and cutting, and I didn't know how to soften them again.

My breath hitched, and another rush of sobs collapsed my lungs. I curled over myself, twisting as small as I could get, like the grief was nothing more than Kyle's questing fists and I could protect my vulnerable organs with my arms and legs.

"You don't strike me as a peppermint tea kinda girl," that annoyingly warm voice intruded again, followed by soft, padding footsteps on the polished floorboards. "So I made you a cup of chai with cream and sugar. I'm more of a coffee guy myself, being from across the Atlantic, but the longer I spend here in England, the more I develop a taste for your leafy stuff."

I tucked my head into my arms, hoping he'd get the message and piss off. But a teacup clattered on the floor beside me, and clothes rustled as if he'd settled against the bookshelves closeby, joints cracking in ... his knees, maybe? How old was he anyway? I hadn't been able to see more than blurs of black, brown, and bright, traffic-cone orange through my tears.

"My name's Brannigan," he said without prompting, his voice a honeyed drawl. "It's a pleasure to meet you, miss."

I half expected him to call me Miss Falcon, but he never finished the name. Coupled with his voice, his accent, and his bearing, that term of endearment made him seem old timey.

"I told you to go fuck yourself," I muttered, my voice thick and raspy, "and it's a *pleasure* to meet me?" I scoffed, wrapping my arms tighter around myself.

"I've caught you at a bad moment," he replied easily, slurping—presumably from his own cup. "I'm not one to judge."

I made a sound in my throat. Everyone judged, whether they admitted it or not.

"I won't hold anything you say today against you," he went on, affable and warm. "And anything you want to talk about won't leave this room, darlin'."

"You're insane if you think I'm going to talk to you," I muttered, wondering if I should stab him just to get him to leave, But he'd probably just 'not judge' me and stay beside me, leg gushing blood. Goody fucking two shoes.

"Well," he mused, his fingernails tapping his cup. "Of course I'm insane; we're all insane in this hall."

That got me to lift my head, and I scrubbed my face clear of tears, narrowing my eyes until I got a good look at him. He was both what I expected and not.

What I expected:

- The lankiness and too-long limbs folded up like an awkward giraffe as he rested his back against the bookshelf
- The bow-tie and violent orange waistcoat
- The thick-framed glasses sitting on his straight nose
- The coaxing smile splitting his rich brown face as he watched me

What I didn't expect:

- Eyes sooooooooooo dark red that he must have been fucking *ancient*

- His stunningly beautiful face, so arresting that my heart skipped a beat
- Cheekbones that could cut the hardest stone, and lips that added a plush, sensual edge to his pretty face
- The drop of blood on the collar of his white shirt, like he'd dribbled his last meal

I stared, blinking hard. "You're a vampire."

Brannigan laughed, a buttery, silken sound that caused goosebumps to rush down my arms. "I know—everyone always thinks I'm a witch. I'm too nice to be a vampire, apparently."

"You're drinking tea," I observed, staring as he took a deep sip. A vampire. Sipping tea. Asking me to talk about my feelings.

What. Was. Happening?

"I am indeed," he agreed with a smile that took up his entire face, his cheeks so squishy and round that his glasses knocked askew. "Anything else?"

"Huh?" I frowned, watching him drain the dregs of his tea with so much baffled confusion it chased away my nightmares.

"Anything else you'd like to remark upon?" He widened his eyes pointedly, but I had no idea what he was talking about. "Ah." He adjusted his bow-tie, something between nervousness and embarrassment crossing his face. "Well, I could always be wrong. That's always a possibility."

"What are you talking about?" I asked, watching him work himself into a panic, his hands fluttering from his bowtie to adjust his glasses, to tweak the buttons on his waistcoat and sleeves.

"Oh, nothing," he laughed, waving a hand. "Don't mind

me, I managed to convince myself of a dream coming to life. A delusion. Are you going to drink your tea?"

I glanced down at the cup he'd set beside my foot and smiled at the cute cartoon kitty on it. "I do like chai," I told him, a tiny olive branch as I lifted the cup to my lips. Oh, it was better than just chai—it was *vanilla* chai.[1] "Thanks," I begrudgingly added, mostly because I could no longer hear Ana's screams in my ears. "I'm Rebel."

"Rebel," he repeated, his warm drawl wrapping around my name like his tongue was making love to it. I flushed, especially as he smiled beatifically at me, a huge beam that bunched his cheeks and bared brilliant white teeth, canines sharp and pointy. "It's a true pleasure to meet you."

"I still think you're mad, Bow-Tie," I said, shaking my head. "But thanks for the drink." I wrapped both hands around the mug and let its warmth seep into me.

Brannigan laughed at the name. "I'm probably being an old busybody, but are you *sure* you don't want to talk about why you rushed in here, crying like you got your heart broken?"

I stared into the pale amber liquid and sighed. "I lost my sister five years ago. Ivelle pried too hard into it, and raked it all up." I shrugged, flippant and defensive at once. "It's not something I want to think about."

"I understand." Brannigan laid a hand on my knee, and I startled at his warm temperature. He must have fed reaaally recently, or gorged on a *lot* of blood to be warm like that. "I've lost people, too. My whole family, as it happens."

My shoulders dropped, sympathy making my heart soft. "I'm not gonna say I'm sorry like dumbasses do, because it doesn't help." I squeezed his hand where it rested on my knee.

"People mean well," Brannigan disagreed. "They just don't know how to help."

"They could try keeping their mouths shut," I muttered, making him laugh that honeyed sound again. It struck me then that we were like one of those cat and dog memes—he was the sunny, optimistic retriever and I was the black cat that hated everyone and shredded furniture with her claws.

He squeezed my knee once more and drew back. "I'll talk to Ivelle, warn her not to push you where it hurts."

I tilted my head, watching as he pushed to his feet in a rush of silk and velvet, all garish colours. "She listens to you?"

"I should hope so, darlin'" he laughed, running a hand over his dark, shoulder-length curls. "I'm the co-founder of Blake Hall."

He smiled deeper as my mouth dropped open, and he chose that moment to finally listen to my demand for space, leaving me to stare after him.

The co-founder of Blake Hall? As in, he set this place up way back when? Holy fuck.

Holy *fuck*.

I'd just had tea with the Blake Hall equivalent of Godric Gryffindor.

19

"Let's try that again," Vivian said in her airy-fairy voice, batting blonde, candy-floss hair out of her face as she gave me a dazed smile. I was ninety percent sure she was high as a kite, her eyes deep blue—like mine—with the pupils blown super wide—*un*like mine.

"I'm doing the best I can," I muttered, sitting opposite her with my legs crossed on the woven rug imported from Thailand or Hawaii or somewhere else she'd gone on her travels. There were photos of her adventures hung on every wall, her face split by a beautiful smile and her arm usually thrown around a broad, blonde guy I assumed was her husband.

"Remember to breathe," she guided, soft and floaty.

"Like I could forget," I said under my breath, fumbling blindly for the place in my blood where my magic was apparently stored, bubbling through my body in every drop. The only glimpse I'd seen had been on the knife when Dean confronted me in the alley. "Alright, now what?"

"Feel for where your magic rushes through you, and lift a hand to it, invite it to present itself."

I closed my eyes, feeling for something that was maybe there, maybe not, and lifted my hand.

"Not your literal hand," she intoned, sounding a lot like a hokey psychic. "Your inner hand."

"My inner hand," I repeated.

"Picture a hand with your mind, and hold it out invitingly to your power," Vivian coached softly, swaying where she sat cross-legged on the floor in front of me, her desk pushed back against the wall for our session.

See, this was why I hadn't made progress with my magic. No offense to hippy, dippy Vivian, but her teaching style was not working for me. I wondered if I could find someone in Mystic Club willing to teach me, but that seemed unlikely. If their head girl—or whatever the whiny blonde actually was—was anything to go by, they wouldn't be too keen to associate with a dual-blood. Especially not a former dud.

But I indulged Vivian's new age teachings, and breathed until my chest rose evenly, picturing a hand held out to my magic—and swearing viciously and creatively when I felt a little tremble inside.

"So you do have magic," Vivian whispered, and I opened my eyes to see the seed of bright silver magic on my fingertip before it faded to nothing.

"Thanks for sounding so surprised, Viv," I huffed, running a hand through my hair. My head was starting to ache from all the exertion. "Glad you believed in me."

"Don't call me Viv," she hissed, her blue eyes flashing suddenly, her placid airiness sharpening. "Only my brother calls me Viv."

I swallowed hard as I leaned away, and wondered if I'd looked like that yesterday when Ivelle pushed for answers about my sister's death. "Sorry," I said genuinely.

She looked surprised at my apology, but only nodded, a

forgiving smile crossing her face and wiping away her grief. I didn't judge her one bit for using drugs to soften her grief; I'd turned to murder for the same reason, after all. "No, I'm sorry," she said with a sigh, her eyes once more hazy. "I'm a little touchy when it comes to my brother."

"How long ago?" I asked. She'd know what I meant.

"A year."

I nodded, compassion rushing up to choke me. "I lost my sister five years ago. She basically raised me; I love her so much. I know exactly how you feel."

Never *loved*. I'd never say love in the past tense, no matter how much people pushed me to move on.

Vivian again looked surprised and offered a smile, moving us away from this topic with a soft, "Reach out to your magic again; it's waiting for your call."

"Here goes nothing," I said, and called to it again.

20

"Dean," I growled, my voice so low and furious I wondered if I might be an alpha female and overpower him until he crashed to his knees.

But my Sexy Sir remained on his feet in the middle of the field behind Blake Hall, his silver hair and broad shoulders framed by the immense cube that had been constructed by magic. Just for us trialists—yippee. As big as a labyrinth and made of thick, dense grass, it looked like a box and a hedge had had a lovechild. Each side had a door. What lay beyond the doors, I didn't know, but Dean warned me this trial would test my power like the other trials had apparently tested my emotional state and physical strength.

Two more trials, and I'd have proved myself to Blake Hall. I'd be allowed to stay. And honestly, as much as it hurt me to admit it, I was starting to like this place. Minus the murder attempts, it was creepy and gothic and I was into that. Plus, my mates were here. Maybe sticking around for a while wouldn't be the *worst* thing in the world. Besides, I was so close to proving my worth, I might as well see it through.

Assuming I didn't get killed first.

"He stays," Dean growled right back, even deeper and more rumbly. I wavered on my feet at his dominance, my wolf whimpering.

But I propped my hands on my hips and gave him my darkest glare. "Are you trying to hurt me, Dean? Because it's working."

His mouth turned down, a sigh expanding his chest as he ducked closer to my glaring face. "I'm not trying to hurt you, baby. But he's your only enemy with access to your trials, and he can hardly attack you if he's busy with his own trial, can he?"

"But," I whined, "I don't want him here." I scowled across the field to where Edison Bray lurked, his icy blonde hair shorn close to his scalp on the sides, showing a vicious black tattoo he didn't have two years ago. He was still devastatingly attractive, but that wouldn't stop me cutting his throat if he so much as looked at me wrong.

"Neither do I," Dean agreed quietly, his expression intense. "But this task is immensely dangerous, and very difficult. There's a chance he could die today." He shrugged, as if he was hoping Bray *would* die.

"But that means I could, too!" I hissed.

"You're too clever and dangerous to die," he disagreed, kissing the spot between my brows. "Time to go, Miss Falcon. Everyone's waiting on you."

"Fuck them. Let them wait."

But I recognised the no-nonsense look that entered Dean's eyes and flattened his expression to pure alpha. I sighed, storming over to my hedge door without even kissing him because I was bitter and pissed off.

"The first task of this trial," Dean said, standing a ways back from the massive cube that stretched six feet above my head, casting a cold shadow that made goosebumps rise on my arms. I'd done the smart thing and worn a jacket today, zipped up to my collar, and I had fluffy pink socks stuffed in my boots in case this trial was as cold as the last two, but I still shivered. More out of unease than chill. I'd known how to face a woods, no matter what creatures roamed it, and the bridge would have been simple if someone hadn't tried to kill me. But this ... what was inside the hedge? "Retrieve the key."

"Huh?" Boyband asked, looking as flawless and celebrity-ish as always. He faced the wall around the corner from mine, staring at it with as much scorn as I scowled at mine. "What key?"

Uh-oh, he hadn't paid any attention to the door in front of him. I hadn't made the same mistake; I'd already scanned the grassy cube before me and spotted the gleam of gold—the lock. Then again, I was used to noticing tiny details in my day job—that's why I'd never got caught as Graves, only as Rebel when I didn't have a clue what I was doing.

I heard the smirk in my Sexy Sir's voice as he said, "*That* key."

I peered over my shoulder and followed his pointed finger all the way up, up, up the grassy cube to where a glimmer of gold caught the dying light. I didn't bother waiting for Boyband or the others to figure out how to get there; I sank my fingers into the turf and discovered a trellis beneath it, buzzing with magic that set my teeth on edge. If I knew how to use my witchcraft, I'd have wrapped a shield around myself to avoid the inevitable hex put on this cube, but I could barely make my fingers spark up. Luckily, all I needed was upper arm strength and determination, and I had enough of both to scale the lower half of the cube, pausing for a millisecond to check on the others. Boyband was just about to jump up, and I couldn't see the other two, but I kept going, putting hand over hand, gritting my teeth against the burn in my muscles, so close I could reach out and—

"You son of a *bitch*," I growled, more than a little wolfy as Edison's tattooed hand snapped the key from its string, dangling it tauntingly in front of my face. I snapped my teeth in his direction, surprised when they were as sharp as Dean's got sometimes, my wolf side surging to the surface. I wondered if my eyes were doing the dark veiny thing, too. Shame I couldn't shift, or I'd claw his face off.

"Too slow, Blossom," he laughed, but the blood drained from his face as the name registered. He hadn't meant to call me that, had he? I stared as he dropped back to the ground, tucking into a ball and disappearing from sight. Shouldn't he have called me *dud* or *failure* or whatever the fuck else he had rotting in that brain of his? Not Blossom, the pet name he'd given me that day two years ago.

"What the fuck?" I breathed, ignoring the wolf's snarl as Vom found the key already gone. I climbed back down, my arms shaking and my mind spinning at a thousand miles per hour.

He hadn't meant to call me that, I knew for sure. But why had the name slipped out? Was that how he thought of me? Even after all these years he'd hated me, rejected me? I wished I'd been strong enough to be unaffected by it—it was probably a mind game he played for fun—but I couldn't help it. Whether he'd rejected me or not, he was my mate, and I was tugged ruthlessly towards him even when I wanted to stab his soft, vulnerable bits.

"Well done, Bray," Dean growled, so deep it was a threat. "You have a minute advantage. The rules of the trial are simple. Inside, you'll find a rotary phone; all you need to do is dial the number thirteen without using your hands, or knees, or elbows, or anything else on your body. This is a test of your mind and your power."

"This is bullshit," Vom snarled, seething with anger. "The witches will clearly win; they're the only ones with magic."

I rolled my eyes. Vom was always whining; I preferred Brunel, but he must have fallen off his bridge and been sent to jail.

"You have dominance," Dean replied coolly. "Wilson has compulsion. Both are kind of power."

"So ... I'm meant to *growl* a phone into submission?" Vom demanded.

Dean's smile was a little mean. "You'll figure it out."

I'd already figured it out. These trials were meant to break us. No wonder there were only three of us left—four if you counted Edison. They wanted to kick us out of Blake Hall, and they'd stacked the odds *way* against us.

I'm not going to fucking prison, I reminded myself. *There's got to be some way to do this. There has to be.*

I had to trust Dean. He wouldn't let me do something that would break me, or separate us.

Right?

"Enter, Bray," Dean commanded, and I heard the tumblers of a lock click into place. And then silence.

A whole minute of silence.

Whatever Edison was doing inside the cube, we couldn't hear a single hint of it. That ... did not bode well. Another shiver went down my arms, and shot up my spine.

"Right, time for the rest of you to go in," Dean rumbled, and lifted a pen. I gave him a dubious look as he held it out in front of him, depressing the button on top, and—three locks tumbled open. Huh. Must have been another witch's charm.

"What happens if we can't do it?" I asked, lifting my hand to press to the cool blades of grass covering the door. This whole thing had to be a witch's creation. Which meant just about *anything* could be lurking inside. A rotary phone for sure ... but what else?

"If you fail the trial, you lose your place at Blake Hall," Dean replied, his gaze practically ordering me not to fail.

I swallowed, pushing the door wider.

That settled it, then. I had no choice but to pass this trial.

21

"This is trippy," I breathed to myself as I stepped into the room beyond the grassy door, my voice amplified and echoed back to me. The creepy vocal equivalent of a hall of mirrors.

I yelped as the door slammed shut behind me, sealing me in with a rustle of leaves. A flash of light surrounded the door, and then ... ah, *shit*. It blended into the wall until there was only a solid block of moss in front of me. There was no way out.

Well, this was fun.

I dug around in my hoodie pocket, taking out a lollipop and sucking it as my anxiety grew. Not even the burst of sweet strawberry on my tongue calmed me as I stared at the room. If it could even be called a room.

Thick-trunked trees stretched from the loamy floor to the black ceiling ten feet above me, the 'sky' twinkling with butter-yellow stars. It was beautiful, but the strangest thing I'd ever seen, and it was *inside a cube*. And it didn't smell of trees or moss or dirt, which was the strangest thing. It smelled of sharp, tangy magic.

The 'room' looked as big as the whimpering wood, but I knew it couldn't have been nearly as vast.

Right?

Fuck, I didn't know anything for sure, and I couldn't take for granted that Dean's involvement in this trial would keep me alive. He'd been fuming and murderous when someone tried to kill me on the bridge, but that didn't mean I could actually do this. And it didn't mean his faith in me was founded. Doubt struck deeper than usual, and I couldn't shake it off, couldn't stop hearing the name Blossom or seeing Edison's stricken face as he dropped to the ground.

Had he already found the phone and turned it to number thirteen? He was the most powerful witch in the Bray line; he'd probably be outside smirking at Dean by now. Smug bastard.

I scanned the trees, the branches spreading out overhead, stars twinkling between them, and I shrugged. There was nothing to do except begin walking, so I patted myself to reassure myself my weapons were still in place, and set off into the trees.

I kept an eye on every branch I passed, waiting for limbs to snap out and snare my waist, hurling me into the air so I couldn't reach the phone. Wherever the phone even was. Every creak of the trees had me stopping and whipping around, and every whisper of wind through leaves had me drawing a knife, sending it hurtling end over end to sink deeply into the bark of a stationary tree.

"I'm going mad," I breathed, and laughed at the absurdity of it. "You think you can break me, grassy cube? Think again. It takes a little more than some ominous rustling to drive me crazy. Because, plot twist! I'm already certifiable."

I stormed on, sucking my strawberry lollipop. "Rebel Falcon, scourge of psychiatrists everywhere. They should put that on my gravestone." I paused, and stabbed my lolly at the trees threateningly. "Don't get any ideas, though; I'm not dying any time soon."

The trees started to thin, but they went on forever and it was getting on my nerves. Where was the damn phone? I had a spot at Blake Hall to defend, and prison to avoid. I could hardly turn the dial to thirteen if there wasn't a dial anywhere nearby, could—oh.

"That's ... not creepy at all," I murmured, sucking hard on my lolly, the strawberry taste my only comfort. Even if I couldn't help tasting magic on my tongue, too.

The trees ended at a perfectly square clearing, the grass cut low and scattered with wildflowers in shades of orange and pink, and right in the middle sat a small, grey table with ornate, curved legs, and a red telephone.

"This is some *Alice in Wonderland* shit," I muttered, scanning the clearing for traps and pitfalls. "And I have no intention of painting roses for a maniacal queen. *I'm* the only maniacal queen around here, all right?" I bit through my strawberry sweet, crunching threateningly at anything that might be listening. I had a feeling I was talking to myself, but the noise helped settle the raw edge of my nerves.

Tucking my clean lolly stick into my pocket,[1] I bent to unfasten my boot and bid it a fond farewell as I lobbed it into the clearing, my breath held in my throat.

"Well," I said, straightening when nothing happened, nothing changing in the weird clearing even a tiny bit. "That's a good sign."

No beasties had rushed out to devour it, no traps sprung or magic zapped my poor pleather sacrifice.

"I knew nothing bad would happen to you," I soothed my shoe as I went to retrieve it, fastening up the laces around my foot. "I wouldn't have let it hurt you, I pwomise."

Drawing a knife, I straightened in the clearing, staring across the few meters between me and the phone. I didn't trust this clearing, with its complete silence—no bird calls, no insects chattering, no rustling leaves. The wind died a few paces back, and the scent of magic was thickest here.

There should have been *some* signs of life, but this place was empty and unsettling, and I proceeded with cautious steps, tapping the grass before I set my full weight down.

Thank kittens there was no countdown for this trial, because I was taking my sweet time, doing every single thing to avoid a trap springing shut. When I finally reached the little wooden table that belonged more in a Parisian house than a magical clearing in a box of grass, I used the tip of my knife to nudge it—and leapt back, braced for explosions and hexes.

"Huh," I huffed, more alarmed at the lack of reaction. "Nothing. Well ... here goes."

Dean had said I couldn't use my body parts; not that I couldn't use a knife, so I used the sharp tip to twist the rotary dial to one, and then to three, smirking as I waited for its reaction.

Electricity crackled up my knife, and I cried out as it sank into my wrist, burning a searing path up my arm and into my chest. I *screamed*, the sound ragged and loud enough to make my own ears ring. Impact rocked up my thighs as my knees hit the grass, and I bowed over my chest as the shock rocketed around, bouncing off my ribs until it finally lost its electric power.

"*Fuck*," I gasped, whined. "Fuck."

I used my good hand to pry my fingers off my knife where they'd locked around the handle, and the solid iron dropped into the grass with a thud. Every breath scalded my lungs, pain stabbing my chest and dragging a whimper from me with every inhale. But no matter how much it hurt, I had to keep breathing.

"Note to self," I gasped, digging my fingers into the grass and pulling up chunks. "No knives."

Which left me with dominance and magic. Great.

I was going to be here a long, long time.

"You can do this," I said weakly, pushing to my feet and gasping through the sharp spasms of pain in my chest. I was going to be having words with Dean about his rules later. He'd never said I couldn't use an object, and as far as I was concerned, this pain was all his fault and he needed to kiss it better. "It's just a phone.

"Just a phone," I repeated, wavering on my feet as I stared down at the red phone, its handset knocked onto the table, connected with a spiral of rubber wire to the base. "It's just a phone."

I didn't know how anyone expected me to growl the phone into submission, so instead I reached for my magic, searching inward like Vivian taught me, and crooked a finger at the tingling power in my veins. A spark rose sluggishly, yet when I opened my eyes, I watched it die out like a sparkler dunked in water. "No!" I pleaded. "No, don't go awayyyyy."

"Ugh," I groaned, and began the process again, my patience already running short. This time, I kept my eyes open, and the second a spark formed, I pushed my hand warily in the direction of the dial ... and watched the seed of light fall harmlessly into the plastic. "Great. Just fucking *great*."

Vivian hadn't taught me how to *do* anything with my power. This wasn't going to work. But I couldn't give up, or I'd a) be murdered in prison by all my enemies, or b) become the bitch of the top dog because I was so cute and infectious. But if I didn't get a move on with b), a) would happen before I could say *I swear to kittens*.

I preferred option c) stay at Blake Hall with my mates and work my way up to become queen of the hall. I could go out murdering on the weekends, spend my days lounging in the window seat in the TV room, and of course my nights would be filled with super hot, mind-blowing sex with my mates. Maybe being a dual-blood was a blessing in disguise. I hadn't exactly been happy in my old life. I'd been alone.

"Like I am right now," I murmured, staring at the phone that just sat there on its table, mocking me. "Okay. Badass witch mode." I dragged in a breath, only slightly flinching with pain as I inhaled, and sank deeper than ever into myself, not opening a coaxing hand but growling a demand at my power, *yanking* at it.

White light flared in my hand, and I growled, my wolf rising in response to the dizziness that made me wobble on my feet. Panting, I guided the white light dripping from my palm towards the dial, snarling at it to turn the dial to one and gasping when it moved with the tiniest little crackle.

"Almost," I breathed, as pain flared in my head, like a little man was trapped in my skull, hammering with his fists to get out. "Almost there." I was nowhere close, but the dial creaked a bit closer to one, and I refused to give up, growling, pulling up more power from inside myself until my hand was overflowing with it.

"Yes," I breathed, when I was halfway there, sweat sticking my shirt to my back under my hoodie, rolling off my forehead. "Almost. So close."

I gritted my teeth at the vicious pain that ripped through my chest, an answering twist in my skull, and I exhaled all at once as the dial nudged to one.

I collapsed to the grass with a sob, pressing my hands to

my face and whimpering at how tender my eyes felt. My eyes ... I dropped my hands and stared at the smears of blood on my fingers.

My eyes were bleeding.

And the itch at my ears told me they were bleeding, too.

This trial was trying to kill me. And it would probably succeed before I ever got that dial to hit three. Nudging it towards one had taken everything from me, made my head pound worse than any hangover, and for a moment I crumpled there and sobbed.

"I can't," I said between broken hitches of my breathing. "I *can't*."

I'd have to resign myself to being someone's prison bitch, because this was impossible. I had scraps of magic at best, and even my growl had only got the dial to one with *immense* effort. I couldn't do this.

The trees rustled suddenly, a sharp wind whipped them into a frenzy, and my head shot up as bright silver light exploded from between a trio of tall trunks. A hole punched through a grassy wall I hadn't even noticed before, and I sobbed as a figure stormed out of it, power rippling off him so strong I shrank back on instinct.

I covered my head with my arms and tucked my face into my knees, shaking all over, pain blasting through my head with every tiny movement.

"These people are fucking nuts," a furious voice spat, and I startled as cool hands lifted my face from my knees, black eyes scanning me and narrowing. "You shouldn't be bleeding."

"Oh, fuck off, Thomas," I snarled, shoving my bastard mate away from me.

"I warned you not to call me that before," he replied, low

and sharp, the wings inked on his throat shifting as he spoke.

"Yeah," I growled, my throat sore with every word. "And you also said you wanted nothing to do with a pathetic dud like me, so why are you here? Get lost."

Edison's black eyes sharpened, his mouth pressed thin, but he didn't back off. He loomed in my personal space, surrounding me with his dark amber scent and his stifling presence. "Don't flinch," he muttered, and lifted his hand, lightning bolts erupting across my jaw as he touched my chin. I jerked back, and he tutted, but his magic sank into my skin and spread crackling coolness throughout my face, through my head.

I waited for my nose to grow, to become a witch's hook, waited for pustules to erupt across my cheeks, but instead my eyes stopped aching, my head stopped pounding, and I felt ... clearer.

"What," I asked, watching his sculpted face suspiciously, "do you *want*, Edison?"

He sighed, looking as pissed off as I did, but he didn't acknowledge my question. "Bring your magic up, and I'll direct it to the dial."

I stayed crouched in the grass as he stood in a fluid movement, rolling up the sleeves of his black shirt. I didn't ask where his jacket had gone, or why there was a slash on his shoulder, interrupting the mermaid inked there.

"Go bother someone else," I muttered, sinking straight into loathing and hurt. He rejected me, had made his feelings perfectly clear; why did he have to rub it in now?

"No attempts to stab me?" he taunted, looming over me with his shiny shoes and pressed slacks and his infuriating smirk. "You're losing your touch, Graves."

I didn't reply.

Edison shrugged, watching me intently. "Your funeral. You'd probably be happier with Anarchy anyway—"

I shot to my feet so fast he couldn't track the movement, and my fist struck his jaw hard enough to bruise my knuckles. I wobbled on my feet, still recovering from the shock to my chest, but it was worth it to see the surprise on his face bleed into—satisfaction? What?

"There you are," he laughed, low and haughty. "Good. Get your magic ready, and let's get the hell out of this place."

"You're helping me," I realised, narrowing my eyes on his sharp, devastating face. "Why?"

"Charity," he drawled.

"Bullshit," I spat, taking a step away from him. "What's in it for you?"

His mouth kicked up into a one-sided smirk, lazy and unfairly hot. I wanted to kick him between the legs, but I'd probably be the one losing my balance and ending up on my ass in the grass. *Later*, I promised myself. My boot, his balls—it was a date.

"Maybe," he said slowly, "I've had an attack of conscience, and I can't bear the thought of my beloved mate so close to death."

I gave him a flat, unimpressed stare. "If you try to kill me, I'll rip your throat out." I reached inside myself for my paltry magic, a low rumble of a growl on the tip of my tongue as I commanded the power to turn the dial.

"Do you have so little power that it's this much of an effort for you?" Edison asked, but not in a sneering way—as if he was surprised.

"Better scraps of power than a dud, right?" I snarled, keeping my gaze narrowed on the phone as white light pooled in my outstretched palm. "If I get shocked for accepting your help, I'll kill you."

"Noted," he replied. And then, "You tried to use your hands too, huh?"

I watched him rub his chest from the corner of my eye, and smirked. "No, my knife. It didn't like that, either. Wow, look at us, being civil to each other. Wonders will never cease," I remarked flatly and jumped as he hovered his inked hands over my magic, drops of his own power trickling down as he shaped and directed the flow of mine. I hated to admit it, but it worked, and with him guiding my magic across the dial, I could focus on letting my magic pour through me and out of my hand.

"That's it, Blossom," he said, and a shiver rushed down my spine at the name in that warm tone. He shouldn't have been calling me that, or talking to me with anything but seething hatred. It confused the hell out of me.

He'd been joking earlier, when he said he had an attack of conscience, right?

"You're at two," he said encouragingly, still a snarling bastard but one who wanted me to succeed.

This was weird.[2]

I reached for more magic, a constant growl tingling my tongue as I pulled up more and more, pain exploding through the front of my skull as Edison guided me.

"So close—there you are—yes!" he exclaimed. "You've done it, Rebel."

That was the first time he'd ever called me by my name. I opened my eyes and swore as I tilted dangerously, dizziness rampaging through my body.

"Why are you like this?" he demanded, catching my arm to steady me. "You shouldn't be this weak."

"I'll ... cut your bollocks off," I rasped, listing into him. Mmm, felt nice being close to him.

Wait no, I hated him.

"You couldn't cut a block of butter, Blossom," he replied with wry humour. "Hold still, I'll heal you again before the door unlocks."

But before he could set his fingers to my face, a sharp whistle split the silence, and our heads jerked up as ropes tumbled from the star-speckled ceiling. I'd seen enough hexes in my life to recognise one on sight.

"Shit," Edison gasped, pushing me away from him as his face turned white. "*Run*, Rebel!"

I fumbled with my feet to follow his advice, but my ankle twisted, the world blurred, and rope lashed around my neck before I could get even a step away.

The phone had been a trigger. A trap.

And now the rope pulled me up into the air, knotted tight around my arms, my middle, and my throat. Grunts and swearing from beside me suggested Edison had been caught too, but I couldn't see him through the veil of my dizziness.

It wasn't a rope around my neck, I realised with slow dread.

It was a noose.

22

*L*ightning-charged magic snapped out around my waist and anchored me to the nearest tree, taking some of the pressure off my neck before it could snap, but I gasped frantically for breath, every exhale a whimper.

I had a pathetic amount of magic, and no way of escaping a hex as bad as this. I felt death creep up on me like a sneaky cat, ready to pounce.

"Breathe, Blossom," Edison snapped.

"I'm—fucking—trying," I replied shortly, scratching at the rope wrapped suffocatingly tight around my throat until I could drag in another wisp of air. "Why don't you—use all that fancy magic—get us free?"

"I'm fucking *trying*," he shot back, and my stomach plummeted like a bungee jumper kicked off a cliff. Not that I'd ever kicked anyone off a cliff. *Ever*.

Edison was one of the most powerful witches of our generation. If he was struggling to fight these magical ropes, there was no hope for me.

"Try harder," I growled, my wolf lashing inside me in a

panic. My teeth ached as canines elongated, but I was bound by the whims of the full moon, and I couldn't shift. Maybe if I was in wolf form, I wouldn't be trapped.

"Rebel, listen," Edison said tightly, and I blinked across the blurring trees to see him struggling against the ropes, bright light surrounding his hands as his magic surged and ebbed. "This seems pretty fucking dire, so I've got something to say."

"Don't," I rasped, tugging at my own ropes and hissed when they didn't budge, just rubbed my fingers raw. If it wasn't for Edison's tendril of magic around my waist, I knew my neck would have snapped and I'd be dead by now. Who the fuck wanted me dead? Oh no, what if that was what Edison wanted to say? What if he wanted to confess to his crimes?

But then why had he raced through the wall to save me?

"Why did you come here?" I asked, my words slow and breathless. "Why do you—care if I—fuck this up?"

Edison snarled, an unimpressive sound after hearing Dean's and Hugh's alpha growls, and he renewed his struggles against the ropes around his neck and chest. "I felt your pain. All right?"

"You felt my pain," I repeated, an irritated rumble filling my voice as my wolf slipped free.

"I felt it through the bond," he snapped, avoiding my glare when I swung around to stare at him, busying himself with the tangle of the knots around his middle.

"That must have,—" I panted, struggling harder as my lungs started to starve of air. "—been inconvenient—for you. I'm *so* sorry."

"Would you shut the fuck up," he snarled, his magic flashing higher, "and let me speak? God, Rebel, you're such a pain in the ass."

"And you're such—a charming gentleman," I hissed back, kicking my legs up until I began to swing, hoping to fray the rope.

"What I wanted to say," he snarled, his black eyes flashing with anger and something else, something darker, "was that I'm fucking sorry. Okay?"

I stopped struggling and stared at him. He had the same icy hair I remembered, the same heavy brow and intense eyes, had that straight nose and cut-glass bone structure, and the same tattoos and deadly aura. But there was no way this man could be the Edison Bray I'd met two years ago. No way in hell would that man have ever apologised. For anything.

"For," I asked slowly, dragging the words from the dark pit of my pain, past all the heartache and misery I'd suffered for years, "*what?*"

His eyes pinched, apology in their dark depths. "You know what my family's like," he said quietly. Not an explanation. "They expect the best, and anything less is a pathetic failure." His bright magic dimmed to pewter at that, as if responding to his thoughts. "I was the golden boy."

"Was?" I cut in before he could go on, frowning at his swinging form. His hair was mussed, and there was a scrape on his jaw, his black shirt smeared with dirt. He looked undone, and I wasn't sure what to make of it. Not that I looked any better.[1]

Edison's low laugh cut the crackling sound of his magic, a laugh full of pain. I frowned deeper, even as I gasped for breath. "I messed up," he said bitterly. "Some asshole tried to steal my phone, so I beat the shit out of him. Got myself thrown in prison for GBH." He laughed again, another bubbling sound of misery and hatred. "I was no longer the perfect heir. They kicked me out."

He shook his pale head, leaning his face against the rope so it cut into his cheek. "You want to know what's seriously fucked up and hilarious?"

"I'm sensing this won't—actually be funny," I panted, watching him in fascination even as I turned lightheaded. I'd never even suspected this Edison existed beneath the asshole; his mask had been complete and without flaw.

"I spent my whole life making sure I was perfect so I lived up to their standards," he said, a sharp smirk curling his lips. "I was terrified as a kid that, if I messed up, if I let the family down, they wouldn't want me anymore. And I was *right*."

I waited for the joke.

Nope, that was it.

"Thomas, that's not funny."

"And that's not my name," he replied, but wryly this time. "I doubt they'll even care when they find out I'm dead. At least now I can't shame the family."

"You're not going to die," I growled, guttural. The mate instincts I'd buried for years came roaring to the surface. He hadn't even said sorry, hadn't said anything that explained why he suddenly gave a shit, but that didn't lessen the force of my need to save him.

I liked to pretend I was violence and sharp edges and ruthlessness, and I was—but it wasn't *all* I was. I was softness and love and loyalty, too. And while I still wanted to cut Edison's balls off for what he'd said to me, for the way he'd treated me, that didn't make my desire to save him from certain death any weaker.

I could chop his balls off later, when we both lived.

Unless he was ready to get down on his knees and ... grovel.[2] Then I might *need* those balls for the future, so I'd leave them attached.

"Pretty sure I *am* going to die, actually," he replied, all bitter and wry. I ignored him; there was no place for pessimism and negativity here. I needed to think of a way out. If these were ordinary ropes, I could do it, even with them around my neck, but they were spelled, and I was fucked.

But there had to be a way.

I refused to die—and I refused to let my mate die.

"They'd have hurt you," he said quietly, without prompting, "and sneered at me. If I'd accepted you."

"Oh?" I demanded, flashing him a glare for interrupting my concentration. "Like you sneered at me? I saw the way you hated me; don't try to convince me you had feeeeelings."

Edison huffed, his bright magic concentrating around the rope at his neck.

"What? No comeback?" I snarked, swinging my legs again. The soles of my boots smacked into the trunk of the tree I'd been strung to. "Fuck," I rasped as I flew out again, the rope pulling taut. On the swing back, I twisted my body around, and ignored the chokehold on my throat as I wrapped my legs around the thick trunk, holding on by sheer thigh power. Good thing I'd kept up my training in my room at Blake Hall, because I was going to need all my strength.

"I'm sorry," Edison said, both hissing and grave. "There was no way I could keep a dud as my mate. *No* way. My family wouldn't have had it; they'd have stripped my heir title from me."

I slammed both hands into the tree and dug in my fingers, bark embedding in my fingernails, eerily scentless.

"Good to know—what's important to you," I gasped, climbing up the tree in tiny increments. A few inches, and the pressure on my neck eased until I could breathe, and I sagged in relief against the trunk.

"And it turns out that title meant nothing," Edison said bitterly. "And the second I messed up, they disowned me anyway."

"Boo hoo," I muttered. "Some of us had bigger problems. Some of us lost their sister in a brutal attack, got viciously rejected by their mate, and went to prison for murder."

"I wanted to keep you," he said quietly. I felt his eyes on my back, but I didn't dare look. The words cut so fucking deep I swore I must be bleeding inside. I sank my teeth into my bottom lip, refusing to cry over this jerk again. "But I *couldn't*, Rebel. We were from different worlds."

"Yeah, I was Juliet, and you were dumbass Romeo," I muttered, climbing higher bit by excruciating bit, until my fingers bled and my thighs *killed*. But I held on, looking for where the noose anchored. If my sparky magic could do nothing else, maybe it could burn through the knot? "I saw the way you looked at me, Edison, and it had nothing to do with your family. You hated me for being your mate."

"I hated *myself* for what I said, for calling you a *thing* when you were the sexiest, most interesting woman I'd ever met. I hated myself for not being brave enough to claim you," he snapped. Pain was heavy in his voice, and I didn't think it was fake.

Chills went down my spine. Was he telling the truth? I wished he was lying, but the words rang true, and everything from that night shifted in a new direction. He hadn't been disgusted with me; he'd been disgusted with *himself*.

Rage burned in my chest—at him, at his family for being judgemental bastards with impossibly high standards, at witch society as a whole. The anger shook in my hands, in my arms, until the back of my tongue tingled with it—and with *power*.

"Shit," I gasped out, recognising the sensation. I'd felt this way when I'd shifted for the first time. "I think I'm going to—"

But my bones snapped before I could finish the sentence, and pain devoured me whole.

23

*A*gony, blinding and complete, was all I knew for minutes, until the sound of fast, panicked breaths filled my ears, and a buzzing rope of something insubstantial wrapped around my middle, just behind my front legs. I gnashed my head, snarling at the glowing silver cord, not fully processing that it was the only thing keeping me from plummeting to my death.

My bones still ached with the memory of snapping and contorting, but I panted through the pain as I gradually adjusted to my wolf form.

"Easy, Blossom," a tight voice said to my right. I snapped my sharp teeth towards the speaker with a menacing growl. "It's me, it's Edison."

I growled louder, deeper. He was the mate who'd rejected me, who couldn't see past his hatred to the person I was. I was more than a magic-less dud, and I would have been well suited to him if he hadn't sneered and insulted me, hadn't cut a wound so deep I hadn't recovered from it in two years.

Don't talk to me, don't even look at me, I roared, but it came out as a garbled mess of snarls instead of words. My wolf's instincts were blurring my brain, and the rejection hurt so much worse in this form. I couldn't think for it, couldn't get past the pain.

"I'll get us down," he muttered, his mouth twisted into a scowl. "You just stay there and growl, yeah?"

I bared my teeth in a threat; he smirked and flicked his hands up at the noose around his throat. If he hadn't had magic, if he hadn't broken through the wall between our trial rooms, my neck would have broken. I'd be dead. But my wolf didn't know that; all she knew was looking at him *hurt*.

"Easy," Edison warned, but he was talking to his power, not to me. Still, I growled deep in my throat, my fur bristling as tingles of cool power filled the space between me and my never-mate. The magic slid over my fur until I was trembling, wrestling against the ropes to get away. No matter how my rational side tried to stop squirming, my instincts were running wild and wouldn't be stopped. I knew the whites of my eyes must be showing.

I was a wolf, hanging twenty feet in the air, bound by hexed ropes and Edison's bright magic. I hadn't thought I'd ever be as scared as that day I'd hidden under Ana's bed, but I was. I was terrified to drop to my death here, or for the noose to snap my neck before I ever reached the ground. I wouldn't even die as a human; I'd die a beast.

"No," Edison rasped, and my head shot up just in time to see a spark of magic race out of control and fray the rope—too fast for my never-mate to react.

Too fast for him to stop his fall.

The animal cry that ripped up my throat was like no sound I'd made before. Crying, I watched Edison plummet to the ground, his pale hands grasping at branches and vines as he passed, and missing every single one. He fell so far that he became an indistinct blur of black ink and icy skin and pale hair, and I waited for his magic to rally, for him to stop his fall. My wolf whined, no longer caring that he'd rejected us, only that he was our mate and he was falling.

But then he hit the ground.

And the sound of bones snapping was the loudest thing I'd ever heard.

What had broken? I twisted against my bindings and cried, desperate to get down, to see how badly he was injured.

Was it his arm I'd heard snap?

Or his neck?

24

*N*o.

No, no, fucking *no*. He couldn't be dead, his neck couldn't have snapped, it *couldn't*.

I choked on a whine with every rasping breath, my wolf form *useless* as I twisted to get free. I didn't have hands with which to climb, didn't have *any* way to get free except uselessly struggling like I was.

The cord of luminous magic around my middle that kept me tethered, stopping my neck from snapping ... it was fraying apart.

I threw my head back and howled, instinct and grief tearing out of my vocal chords in a melancholy cry.

He couldn't be dead. He was Edison fucking Bray, the golden boy of the Bray line, one of the most powerful witches in our generation, and the most smug, infuriating, cocky prick I'd ever met. He was sharp, and darkly funny, and dangerous, and—

He was my mate. And he was dead.

I howled louder, my heart ripping out of my chest, and —something else swelled in my chest, too, something as effortless as breathing, a power that answered the summons of my howl. This was nothing like the power I'd dragged out of myself to get the dial to turn; my ears didn't bleed, and my head didn't pound. This poured out of me like a waterfall, like a storm, and only did damage to everything it came into contact with *outside* me. If anything, I felt stronger. Clearer. Like I'd been given a glass of cool water after weeks of thirst.

I took a deep inhale, and exhaled power. It didn't matter that the tether around my middle winked out, because my own magic held me aloft. I was a dud, a failure of a witch, but there was no denying the immense power that disintegrated the nooses, turned the hex on the rotary phone to dust, and lowered me gradually, carefully to the ground like I was freaking Supergirl.

I had half an inkling that I was subconsciously controlling the magic with my mind, but it felt like a benevolent god lifted me gently to the ground, placing me within reach of Edison.

I took a rushed step towards my broken mate, but I paused at the sight of my huge paw on the ground. It was four times the size my paw had been when I'd shifted before, it was silver—not black—and it was *glowing*.

And ... and we weren't anywhere near the full moon.

What the hell was happening? Had I used magic, somehow, to force a shift? Huh. It looked like I'd found the dual-blood cheat codes. I'd contemplate everything about that later.

Now, I hurried over to my mate and collapsed to the grassy floor with a loud thud that set the trees quivering. Oops. I was still getting used to being fucking *enormous*. Was I bigger than Hugh would be as a wolf? I didn't know what I'd done with my magic, but it didn't matter. All that mattered was Edison, limp and unconscious on the ground.

Unconscious—

Wait. I tilted my huge head, pricking my ears. Yes, there was a heartbeat. And the faint, jagged sounds of his breathing.

I slumped forward with relief, my bristling fur settling back into place down my spine. He might have had broken bones, but he was alive. There was hope. I just had to get him out of here and to a doctor. He'd be fine. He'd be okay.

He had to be.

I leaned closer to lay my head on his chest, the only way I could assure him he'd be alright, but I paused at the trickle of scent clinging to him. No, clinging to the *noose*, and to the ropes still twisted around his body.

As a regular wolf, the trace had been too faint for my nose to pick out, but with magic supersizing me and my senses, my nose twitched. Something was familiar about the scent. There was magic there, remnants of the hex, and the signature of a witch I didn't recognise, but there was ... family.

I reared back with the realisation, a deep rumble in my chest making the leaves quake around us. Yes, there was no doubt at all. Whoever had strung these hexed nooses in the trees shared blood with me.

My own family was trying to murder me. They'd almost succeeded three times now. But harming Edison ... that was going too far.

I was going to hunt them down, peel their skin from their bodies, and crush their bones to ash.

While they were still alive.

And if Edison *didn't* survive ... worse. My wrath would be so. Much. Worse.

The world had better watch its fucking back. Rebel "Graves" Falcon was on the warpath.

THANK you for picking up Killer Crescent - I hope you loved Rebel and her men! There is wayyy more blood, gore, murder, and steam coming in book two, Blood Wolf. It releases in Late Autumn 2021.

You can let me know you love the series by leaving a review of this book, and preordering the next one.

Thanks for the support you've shown Rebel so far—it means the absolute world to know how you love her twisted, psycho heart of gold as much as I do <3

Leigh

THANK YOU FOR READING!

Need the next book ASAP? Let me know – the more demand for a series, the more likely I am to bump the next book to the top of my list! To stay updated with what I'm working on next, come join me in my Paranormal Den on Facebook, or sign up to my fortnightly newsletter! (Links on the next pages, so keep reading, loves.)

If this is your first Leigh Kelsey book, I have lots more books for you to sink your teeth into, and four completed series. I've got vampires, wolves, shifters, angels, and demons - and of course plenty of growly alpha males with tragic backstories

Reviews make the world go 'round - or at least they do in my world. If you loved this book and you can spare a minute, please leave a review on Amazon or wherever else you like to review. Even the smallest, one-line review has an impact, and helps me reach new readers like you awesome people.

Thank you to everyone who's already reviewed. Your words mean I can keep writing the books you love!

A REVERSE HAREM FAE ROMANCE

New Series!

INSPIRED BY HADES & PERSEPHONE

THREE SWOON-WORTHY LOVE INTERESTS AND NO CHOOSING

A KICKASS WOMAN WITH MAGIC

A MAGICAL, SWEEPING STORY OF MAGIC, FATED MATES, AND FOUND FAMILY

A SLOW-BUILD PLOT OF DARKNESS AND TWISTED MONSTERS

SLOW BURN ROMANCE THAT'S HOT IN THE NEXT BOOK

I hope you'll join me on my next magical adventure, with a kickass, magic-wielding main character, fae and shifter fated mates, and an epic world full of monsters, saints, and power!

Read free with Kindle Unlimited!

JOIN MY READER GROUP!

Join my reader group for news, giveaways, and exclusives!

To get news about upcoming releases before anywhere else, and early access to my books, come join my Leigh Kelsey's Paranormal Den group over on Facebook!

THREE FREEBIES FOR YOU

Join my newsletter for 3 exclusive freebies!

Fancy some freebies? I'll send you three when you join my newsletter! I promise never to spam you, and I rarely send more frequently than once a fortnight so you won't be overloaded with emails.

Join here: http://bit.ly/LeighKelseyNL

COMPLETE RH WOLF SHIFTER SERIES!

Having every male werewolf in the area lining up to claim you might sound like a good thing, but belonging to a wolf is Lyra's worst nightmare. Too bad she's about to belong to three.

READ FREE IN KINDLE UNLIMITED

COMPLETE RH ANGEL/DEMON FANTASY SERIES!

Betrayed by heaven, protected by hell. The devil and his hellhounds will do anything to keep their angel safe.

READ FREE IN KINDLE UNLIMITED

COMPLETE RH DRAGON SHIFTER SERIES!

They cuffed her.
Branded her.
Locked her up, and threw away the key.
But Trouble won't let these a*holes break her.

READ FREE IN KINDLE UNLIMITED

COMPLETE RH VAMPIRE SERIES!

A blood-drenched legacy. Three devoted lovers. An ancient evil rising.

Elara will be lucky to survive her new life as a vampire...

READ FREE IN KINDLE UNLIMITED

ABOUT THE AUTHOR

Leigh Kelsey is the author of sweet and steamy books for anyone with a soft spot for steely women and the tortured men who love them. No matter what stories she's writing – vampires or shifters or rebels – they all share a common thread of romance, heart, and action. She is the author of the Lili Kazana series, the Vampire Game series, the Moonlight Inn series, and the Second Breath Academy series. Leigh also writes new adult and young adult books under the name Saruuh Kelsey.

FIND THESE OTHER BOOKS BY LEIGH KELSEY!

All solo books free on Kindle Unlimited*

Bargain Box Sets

Call of Magic (99c Paranormal, Urban Fantasy, and Fantasy stories)

Fae of the Saintlands series

Heir of Ruin

Heart of Thorns

Kiss of Iron

Rebels and Psychos Duet

Killer Crescent

Blood Wolf

Broken Alphas series

The Omega's Wolves

A Feud So Dark And Lovely series

The Goblin's Bride (99c preorder - MF Enemies-to-Lovers Fantasy Romance)

Blacktower Prison for Supernaturals series

(complete series)

Prison of Embers

Tower of Sparks

Fortress of Flame

Refuge of Firelight

Lili Kazana series
(complete series)
Complete Series Box Set
Cast From Heaven
Crowned By Hell
Called By Gods

Vampire Game series
(complete series)
Complete Series Box Set
Vampire Game
Vampire Touch
Vampire Legacy

Moonlight Inn series
(complete series)
Complete Series Box Set (w/ exclusive epilogue!)

Mated

Empowered

Unlimited

Ascended

Unleashed

Victorious

Dead Space Universe

Dead Space (RH Sci-Fi Stand-Alone)

Second Breath Academy series

How To Raise The Dead

How To Kill A Shadow

How To Banish Evil (Coming Summer 2021)

Stand Alone Stories

Sinful Beauty (RH Demon Romance Stand-Alone)

*Moonlight Inn temporarily un-enrolled from the Kindle Unlimited program

FOOTNOTES

Chapter 1

1. I was ninety percent sure it was the pink hair.
2. Not together; I wasn't a monster.

Chapter 2

1. Was a doughnut without sprinkles even a doughnut?

Chapter 4

1. Dean had refused to let me put Britney on. Killjoy.
2. Be mature, Rebel, you're a grown adult woman who will *not* snort at the word knockers.
3. Pun intended.
4. —ter. Made me wet*ter*. All his fault, of course.
5. I pouted again; he pointedly ignored me.
6. If perfectly respectable young ladies had hot sex in cars with dominant alpha strangers.

Chapter 5

1. Note to self: step out of line at first opportunity.
2. Dibs.
3. Booooring.
4. The window seat was mine now. Fight me, bitches.
5. And for a hobby, let's be real, murder was fun.
6. Why were assholes always so tall? And hot? Fuck them all. Wait, not literally!
7. But it *did* hurt. It thrust a serrated knife into my heart and cut it in two.
8. Uhh, wolf hug?

Chapter 6

1. Or the second film for the heathens who haven't read the books yet.
2. I honestly could not tell you his name, or how he was related to me. Let's call him John.
3. Or Dave, or Bob.
4. Again.
5. Or Phil, or Nigel.
6. Or Charles, or Trevor.
7. Because I was a *lady*.
8. My pussy clenched around his cock as my head fell back on a groan. Oopsie.

Chapter 7

1. Who needed carved wooden boxes for their tissues? And to think that people called *me* odd. They ought to meet rich people.
2. Alright fine, I still liked to rip the heads off my Barbies and kick boys in the playground.
3. And stomped on it, and crushed it beneath his shiny shoe, and then spat on it for good measure, all while wearing that smirk that made me want to punch his damn lips off his stupid, beautiful face.
4. Why did I want to get bitten? Seriously, why? What was wrong with me? Wait, don't answer that.
5. Maybe because I wanted his fangs buried inside me as much as I wanted his cock. Self preservation instincts, what self preservation instincts?
6. Gift cock?
7. Was it normal to be sucking the neck of someone I'd just met?
8. Dean was in denial, but he'd wake up soon.
9. Note to self: employ a cleaner.

Chapter 9

1. Not that I liked caviar. Gross.

Chapter 10

1. More. Wobbled more. I was already close to falling over.
2. Like a guide dog, but fangier.

Chapter 11

1. My perfume was called Cupcake Couture, and yes I did blend it myself because nothing else was sweet enough for my saccharine tastes.

Chapter 12

1. 99.9999999999999999999999999999999999999999 and a few extra 999999s for good measure.
2. Whatever the fuck they even were.
3. Althoughhhh.... that sounded kinda fun. Note to self: learn murdery magic.
4. And avoiding any exciting areas juuuuuust in case I needed that in the future.

Chapter 13

1. And when a crazy person goes crazy, you know things are bad.
2. I'd told Ivelle what my scary stalker had said, but do you know how many blonde-haired women my size there were in the world? Hell, there were sixteen of them just in Blake Hall. Boo!

Chapter 14

1. Self-care is suuuuuper important, guys. Don't neglect your mental health, even if it means finding some douche to bury six feet under.
2. Errr... paranormal beings.
3. And no, for once I didn't mean a thick, mouth-watering cock.
4. I'd called her Tina. No particular reason; she just felt like a Tina to me.
5. I preferred him un-stabbed. If he was stabbed, we couldn't have sexytimes.

6. Hot manly groans > breathing.
7. And turned me allll the way on. And I couldn't even be held accountable for this questionable life choice, because it was all my body's doing. That whore.

Chapter 15

1. Translation: back off my woman, you giant, oozing pustule.
2. Another normal person reaction! I was *nailing* this rehabilitation!

Chapter 16

1. I'd let him stroke my pussy anyday.
2. Okay fine, you caught me. I was staring *hard*. I'd memorised every single muscle packed on his body like I was revising for a test.
3. He... might not fit. Just a hunch.
4. Even though I wasn't...
5. Well, he ducked; I just walked forward.
6. Shame I couldn't upload that software to regular men. I'd make a killing selling it to their wives.

Chapter 17

1. But was there reaaaaally ever a bad time for desk sex, I ask.
2. It's a word. Look it up, folks.

Chapter 18

1. AKA ambrosia of the gods. I'd kill for a box of this stuff most weeks.

Chapter 21

1. I might be a crazed lunatic, but there was one thing more heinous than murdering arseholes: littering. Don't do it, kids, save the planet and all that jazz.
2. Back me up—this was weird, right?

Chapter 22

1. I was ninety percent sure I had a branch in my hair. Not a twig; this baby was too big to be called a twig.
2. What did you think I was going to say? Tssskk, dirty minded!

Printed in Great Britain
by Amazon